Reading *As If Place Matters* is like venturing into the Twilight Zone. When you read Juhasz, be prepared to be transported to those thoughts only hinted at when in the company of those we trust. You know, where our minds ponder questions not intended for the faint of heart. Juhasz's narratives suggest that it is not all random coincidence; maybe it is selected patterns moving us forward. Those narratives woo us to greatness by asking us to swallow the trumpeted spittle of the masters so that we may absorb their courage. They ask us to cuddle with hitmen. His stories reveal the monsters around us and within us, and they have us march to false patriotism, where childhood is stolen for the sake of bragging rights. Juhasz has us understand that our inner rōnin can be a blessing or curse depending on perspective. He truthfully ponders the depths of boyhood friendships and finds them lacking. He shows us the minute details that matter and challenges the most crucial question—does love matter?

So set aside your fears, or better yet, race toward them and wait for the bottle rockets to go off.

Woodstok Farley, Author of *The Water Stop Saloon*

As If Place Matters:
Short Fiction

Paul Juhasz

First published by Fine Dog Press 2023

First edition
ISBN: 978-1-955478-21-2

For Ky,
who kept me alive.

"Great was that chase with the hounds for the
unattainable meaning of the world."

Czeslaw Milosz

Table of Contents

Appalachian

"Shipwrecks are *apropos* of nothing."
Stephen Crane

1

Michael Kroening drives into the late-afternoon spring Texas sun. His body on auto-pilot, mind untethered, floating in his own little world. The scrub oak and Tex-Mex chains visual white noise working with the rhythmic hum of tire on patchwork asphalt. What mental attention Michael has is focused backwards; on the lunch at Pappadeaux's and the virtually-closed deal; and forward, on thoughts of commission and on the used bass-boat the commission will become.

He sees the motion, peripherally, well before his mind attentions it. Even then, he has a hard time processing. The over-sized semi tire, galvanized rubber and steel cords, has already bounced across the eastbound lanes, is nearly across the ryegrass and wildflower median, is on a collision-course with Michael's battered 4Runner. There is no truck in sight in either direction. Just this tire, untethered, hopping playfully like a wayward marble.

Unreasoning, random, inevitable, the tire bounders on as Michael watches. The mind is no help. All it offers is the briefest memory of lunch, a faint whiff of shrimp brochette, how the charred bacon almost but not quite crowded out the pungency of jalapeño.

Michael just watches, as the tire, its predictable path unpredictably altered by a chance jog to the right, misses the inches of his rear bumper, disintegrating the windshield and driver of the car behind him.

Michael does not stop.

He lives out his life of average mundaneness until heart failure calls him at seventy-eight. Occasionally during the intervening forty-four years, Michael remembers the tire, its random concentration. He recollects shards of glass and steaming strips of rubber, gives a moment's fleeting thought to the obliteration of the driver who let Michael merge ahead of him a mile back.

Michael is not prone to much speculation, so in these moments, it does not occur to him to wonder which the intended timeline and which the stolen? Which life the boon of a few seconds in either direction?

2

The dryer-chair was always Rita's favorite part. While she liked Roseanne well enough, and she appreciated that Marlene and Julie—the other two stylists at Regal's Salon—never seemed resentful that she didn't prefer them, and while Leo, the owner, was always so polite and charming, such a nice change of pace from what she got at home from Jim, there was always something so banal, so superficial and fake about the conversations they had. Like when someone asks, "How are you?" and you just know they're not listening to your reply, the question a mere formality. Sometimes she thinks about telling them, "Jim took the phone book to me again last night," just to see how they react.

But within the bubble of the chair, a contained atmosphere, humid, prehistoric, and pure, Rita felt soothingly alone. Safe in her isolation, she'd hold a magazine, rhythmically turning the pages, not reading the articles, just looking at the ads and the promises they contained, the perfect worlds they implied. Each, a place where she longed to fit. A beach, a high-brow cocktail party, Paris. Fanciful places. Without phone books. Without Jim or his friends; the ones he likes to share her with, the ones she was expected to cook dinner for, and then let them do whatever they wanted after. Sometimes they'd go at her so hard for so long that she would have trouble sitting down for days. Without Jim's jeers: "If you don't like all the attention you get, I can always get rid of ya and find someone who will. I'll get Rita you. Get it? Get Rita you." And he'll laugh that gap-toothed fog of old-coffee-and-fresh-whiskey laugh. Or he'd remind her that if she left, she'd be alone for the rest of her life. "Who the hell's gonna want you? Middle-aged woman rode hard and put away wet?"

Rita believes this is true, so she stays and dreams into advertisements.

"This is as close as I'm ever going to get to NASA, I'm afraid." The voice breaks into her daydream. A strange new voice. Male. A light orange-and-yellow button-down shirt opened to the fourth button. Two gold necklaces and a medallion nestled in a garden of twisted black chest hair with subtle whispers of grey. And light blue eyes coring right through her.

Rita blinked in wonder.

"I don't think they let men like me in," he whispered into her silence.

Rita knew what he meant by "men like me." Jim would call him "a faggot." But looking at him seated under the dryer, the only word that came to Rita's mind was "flamboyant." She reflexively winced at the word choice, knowing how much Jim hated it when she used fancy words like that. Not knowing what else to say, she offered, "I don't think I've seen you here before."

"Oh, Lord, no, sugar," he said with exaggerated disgust, like she just suggested he eat a live, still wriggling, caterpillar. "I'm just a friend of Leo's. I'm on tour. We just did a show in Indianapolis and we head to Detroit tomorrow, but I haven't seen Leo in *for-ev-er*, so I just had to drive over. I'm Marcus," he introduced with a limp handshake. "Like Marcus Aurelius, the philosopher-emperor."

The handshake was also exaggerated, overdone, cliché. Rita was surprised to find that's what she immediately liked about Marcus. His exaggeration seemed intentional, a parody of expectation, holding within itself a craftily-hidden rejection, a refusal to conform to space, to wear it, mockingly, as a thin veneer. Protected within this pushback, he maintained his own space, his own little world, carried it with him wherever he went. Rita did not understand how she immediately recognized this; she just knew she found herself suddenly refreshed.

"Oh, look at the big grin on you, girl! But I must tell you, that," Marcus pointed at the magazine open on her lap, at the image she had been transfixed by before he spoke, a forest, lush and green, "that's not the place for you. No, Sugar. When you leave him, don't go there?"

"Where should I go, then?" she surprised herself with the reply.

Marcus stared at her for several beats, those blue eyes absorbing, dissecting. "San Diego. San Francisco. Maybe Seattle."

"I have family in Chicago."

"Oh, *puh-lease*! Not Chicago. Nah-nah. You ain't Chicago. You ocean. Ocean wipes away. Ocean gives back, each wave a possibility. When you're ready to go, get you some ocean. If you go east, what you get is an ocean, ancient and sage. But it's willful, tumultuous. West is young, tempestuous. And fickle."

After a pause, he continued, "Mountains can work the same way. There's wisdom in mountains too, pushed up from the earth itself, that we can tap into. But you're not mountains, Sugar; you're ocean."

"I also have family in Galveston."

Marcus just looked at her for a while, his expression one of weary resignation, the look of one having to explain something very simple to someone very young. "Ocean, Baby. Not gulf. Ocean."

"How do I know which one? East or west?" Rita asked, surprised at how quickly the idea of leaving Jim had become an open conversation.

"It don't matter which. Both do their job. The going's the important part. Just as well flip a coin." Marcus reached into his pocket, pulled out his hand and enfolded Rita's in it. Turning her wrist over, he pried her fingers open, letting the quarter fall into her palm. "Either is better than where you are now. Right, Sugar?"

When Rita nodded, Marcus stood. Rita was shocked at how tall he was, as if he did not so much stand as unfurl.

"I'm dry enough now. It was *such* a pleasure, Rita. You flip that coin now, you hear? Most people, they don't worry about the collisions; they just collide. So you flip that coin." He leaned in to hug her, and once again Rita surprised herself by hugging him back, hard, familial. It never dawned on her to ask how he knew her name. Marcus turned his head, whispered in her ear, "And if you don't like how the coin flips, there's always the other side."

Rita sat there for several minutes after Marcus left, staring at the coin in her hand. Jim was down state, hunting with his cousins near Spencer Township. Rita had been anticipating his return with dread and anticipatory shame, knowing how she'd be expected to greet their return. Now, she thought, that trip could be her salvation. She could drain the savings account and go. It'd be two days before Jim would know.

Rolling the quarter between her fingers, she assigns values. Heads, she goes; tails, she endures. Before she flips, she recalls what Marcus whispered to her and knows the flip doesn't matter. The flip is not the randomness. But she smiles and decides to flip the coin anyway. Just for form's sake.

3

There is no reason for Marcel to be up. He is not ill; he did not wake from a bad dream, nor—since he has no wife, no children, no obsession with things—is he beholden to a world of worries. He is secure, self-contained, and content. He is just unaccountably, atypically restless. At 2:00 in the morning, Marcel decides to grab a smoke on the balcony, and adds the annoyance of being out of cigarettes to the annoyance of sleeplessness.

After a moment's thought, Marcel shrugs into a light jacket and heads for the Turkey Hill on the corner, buys a pack of American Spirits and steps back outside.

Marcel cups his hand behind his lighter and flicks the sparkwheel once, twice, five times without getting a flame that can defy the steady breeze. Annoyed again, he walks around the corner, using the store as a windbreak.

Before he can try the lighter again, he hears a metallic thud, laughter, and muffled voices. He listens a few moments more, parses the noises out. One is female and fear-laden. Marcel is no hero, but he walks to the opposite corner, peeks around to the back of the store.

Most of the scene is blocked by the two green Dumpsters, but what Marcel can see paints a clear enough picture. Bare legs, between them blue jeans pooled just above knees and a pale white ass plunging forward, over and again. Standing just behind, in full view of Marcel, a college-aged boy, watching, rubbing the crotch of his jeans in slow, sweeping circles, waiting his turn.

"C'mon," the standing boy says, "hurry up. I want my turn too. And Brad still hasn't gone. I still get to go next, right, Brad? You said I could be next."

"Yeah," a voice from behind the Dumpster replies. "You go after Todd finishes. But you better pull out before you cum. I ain't sticking my dick in a chowder pot."

The standing boy giggles the giggle of the simpleton. "Maybe I'll cum on her face, like in those movies."

"Whatever you like," Brad replies.

Because the standing boy turns his attention back to Todd, Marcel finds himself doing the same. Todd's thrusts, his grunts, her muffled screams, her crying, in symphonic accord.

Marcel steps back behind the corner and flicks the sparkwheel repeatedly without result. Annoyed yet again, he holds the translucent blue up to a streetlight's glare and sees only a hint of fuel remaining. He tosses the useless lighter to the asphalt, takes the cigarette from his mouth and ponders it. From around the corner, the giggling of a simpleton has been replaced by the grunts of one. Todd, Marcel notes, has finished.

He rolls the cigarette between his fingers, thinking, then pivots back towards the entrance, where he buys a replacement lighter and makes a mental note to get better at checking the fuel level next time.

Back at his apartment, he smokes one on his balcony and heads back to bed, where he is soon asleep, secure, self-contained, and content.

4

The tornado touched down in a field of red clay and scrub thirteen miles from town. When the National Weather Service issued its warning, it was already rated an F3 on the Fujita scale. As it plowed its way northwest, it grew in size and intensity, a churning wedge-shaped F5 monster that one local meteorologist referred to as "The Hammer of God."

Before the behemoth dissipated, it had taken the town of Clear Springs with it entire. Twenty-three people were killed. Every structure in the town, every home, every store, every school, the hospital, the YMCA, every restaurant, every church, Planned Parenthood, an entire little world, was gone. Erased. Every structure, that is, except the house at 16 N 2nd St, which had been miraculously bypassed. The house at 10 N 2nd St had been disintegrated down to its foundations; the word the All-State insurance agent used to describe the house at 22 N 2nd St, was "obliterated," but the tornado jumped Harlan Owens's ranch house completely.

Asked to account for this, to explain how his house lost nary a shingle while every other person in town lost everything, Harlan Owens can only shrug his shoulders and ruminate a moment or so before concluding, "Just God's will, I suppose."

5

There is a field. A field resplendent with fern and nascent angiosperm, edging up to seemingly endless coniferous forest, lush and green. In this Cretaceous savannah, herds of hadrosaur, ever watchful for predators, roam, taking care to stay away from the handful of cantankerous triceratop grazing about. In a sea nearby, mosasaurs chase shark and ray while in the skies above, pterosaurs soar on currents of warm air, only tangentially concerned with terrestrial matters. On a branch of a primitive pine at the tree line, a cimolodont barks, scolding the larger animals in the field before it, and is ignored.

A yearling hadrosaur wanders off from the group. too focused on forage to notice its separation. The rest of the herd also does not notice the wandering, too focused on their own narrow concerns, the biology of provender and gestation. The yearling's straying *has* been noticed, though. From the tree line, a small pack of raptors track it, coordinating their attack with clicks and chirps.

A blindingly-bright streak rushes across the sky, its lagging roar causing the hadrosaur herd (except one) to lift theirs heads in jittery panic. There is a concussive crash, the ground rumbles, a wall of force and heat incinerate everything in sea and sky, forest and field. A heat so intense it melts rock. Sulfur and carbon dioxide vaporize, fall as glass-like spinels, fuse with magnesium, iron, and nickel, blending with iridium from the asteroid itself. Over time, water fashions this chemical cocktail into a thin strip of clay that whispers the story of a force 500,000 times greater than any atomic bomb, of apocalyptic darkness and mass extinction, for any who care to read.

6

Michael Kroening sits on the edge of a neon-blue Adirondack, holds a sweating bottle of Shiner Bock. He is staring into the sky, watching a lingering contrail highlighted against cerulean, and hopes Wilson won't tell the story. All the while *knowing* Wilson will tell the story. Wilson, Michael's long-time friend, has his own "just-missed" story. Tells it every cookout. Stands in the humidity of the back yard, wrapped in a cloud redolent of charred meat and lighter fluid that the insistent Texas wind can only partially disperse, affectedly clears his throat and begins his performance. "Did I ever tell you," he'll ask, and without awaiting a response, plows into it. About his wife, Gloria. How he was running late, driving too fast, almost hit a squirrel.

"But you don't really hit a squirrel, do you?" Wilson chuckles on cue, flipping the burger, turning the brat. "The squirrel hits you. Just up and decides one day that a life of hoarding nuts no longer satisfies. Or maywise, it can no longer deal with the fact that, despite that elegant tail, it's still just a rat. So, the squirrel wants out. And you just happen to be driving by, right on cue. Then, bam!

Without any volition or decision on your part, you get roped into this damn squirrel's suicide."

After whatever laughter is offered—polite snorts from new guests who are appreciative of his largesse (for Wilson is a gracious host) or wearied, good-natured groans from veterans like Michael who have heard all of this before, many times, Wilson continues with the story. How he parked slantwise, taking up three spaces. How he "raced" across the parking lot (although, it is clear looking at Wilson that "raced" is an extravagant choice of verb). And then the decisive moment of worlds colliding: how Gloria hit him with the door as she exited, he entered, the podiatrist's office.

Wilson will then sigh, look off wonderingly, milking the moment, staging his final pronouncement: "If I didn't run that last yellow light, I'd have missed out on everything. I'd never have found my gold." He'll stroke Gloria's blonde hair as he says this last. Because he is content, Wilson will never consider what he may have gained elsewise, now lost, unremarked.

7

Father Shea awoke to the chirping of the machine next to the bed tracking his heart rate, his blood pressure, to the metronomic drip of the IV. He smiles weekly at the sight of Agnes, ever-devoted Agnes, the self-appointed sentinel. No one in his parish could rival her concern.

When he initially became ill, when the palsies could no longer be chalked up to the inheritance of old age, Agnes was there, driving him to check-up after check-up. When the bulls-eye shaped rash on his legs and back were explained, when the doctors spoke of *borreliosis*, Agnes was there. And when his damaged heart brought him to Intensive Care, Agnes came too. She watches him sleep. She prays, rolling her rosary through her fingers like a boy working marbles. She sees—over-sees, Father Shea sometimes thinks to himself—to his needs during the few hours he is awake.

He used to think of Agnes as one of the Pharisees, her concern, affectation; her care, performance. Now, as he nears the end, he finds he does not care. He is glad not to be alone. He listens to her silently for a few moments. She is reading from her dog-eared and worn Bible. Psalm 23.4, predictably. When he was young and first took orders, Father Shea always found that passage so bleak and melodramatic. Now he finds it, like Agnes's presence, comforting.

"Hello, Agnes."

"Oh!" Agnes startles. "How are you, Father Shea?"

"I'm fine, Agnes. Fine."

"Can I get you anything?"

"No, Agnes."

Agnes is silent a moment, preparing to start the exchange that has become ritual, a litany.

"Everyone in the parish misses you, Father Shea. We don't understand why this has to happen. To you of all people."

Father Shea offers a weak smile and delivers his lines. "It's just God's will, Agnes. We need not question it."

He is not just offering Agnes a platitude for comfort; Father Shea has always had a deep-seated conviction in God's plan. From when he first heard the calling to this very moment, struggling against the ravages of a bacterial infection with a weakened heart, Father Shea has always believed there was a plan, a narrative, that explained all things, even—in fact, especially—the unexplainable. Something as basic as his potential death after more than eight decades in the Lord's service was just a minor part of this great narrative. He reaches over and pats Agnes's hand and then holds it for a little while.

Later that night, when Father Shea passes, an indecipherable smile records his final moment. Was this the beatific smile of the justified? Or appreciation for a really good joke, well-told? No one, not the doctor plodding through his rounds that night, not the nurses flitting in and out of the room, nor Agnes, loyal to the end, could say for certain.

8

Far out in space, well past Mars, an endless sea of asteroids float and bob, a planetesimal band of kinetic possibility.

9

1966 was a brutal summer to be a baseball fan in Chicago. On July 13, the Cubs were 26-57, firmly vectored toward last place. The White Sox were not much better at 38-47-1. Most of the drinkers in the Shipyard Inn tavern are complaining about this as they down cold beer to combat the 87-degree mugginess. Despite their complaints, they fervently wish the Cubbies and the Sox were playing today.

Those that aren't nagging baseball are peddling their outrage over last night's riots in West Town. They assume Officer Munyon was justified to shoot that spic kid, think Arcelis Cruz ("And what the hell kinda name is 'Arcelis?'" they grumble) should be thankful the bullet only hit his leg. They have little sympathy for the three thousand Puerto Ricans protesting on Division Street right now as they sip their beers. They say things like, "If they don't like it here, they can go back where they came from," as if place mattered. These people also wish there was a baseball game in Chicago today.

But not Elie Mae Hooper. She is not thinking about baseball as she drinks at the bar in the Shipyard Inn tavern. Nor is she thinking about last night's riot, nor the one looming today. Elie Mae Hooper is just getting hammered, trying her hardest to think of nothing, a word that perfectly describes how she sees her prospects for love and attention as a fading flower of fifty-three.

And not the young man sitting on the stool next to her, who has bought her last three rounds. The young man with the wavy dark-blonde hair and the dull hazel eyes, the tattoo on his arm that reads "Born to Raise Hell." He's thinking about that bitch, Shirley, back in Texas. How she dared to file for divorce. She was *nothing* when he found her, wandering aimlessly through the midway at the State Fair, just another whore, another vessel. And although Richard Speck preferred his whores older, like this one sitting beside him, he made the decision to bestow himself upon this lost, wandering fifteen-year-old.

And "bestowed" was the right word, Speck thought. For he was a gift. Nothing less than. But did Shirley appreciate this gift? Was she grateful? When, in just three weeks the field was sown and she was with child, did she appreciate *that* gift? Was she grateful then? No. Shirley—that ungrateful bitch whore—just nagged. Nagged about him being in and out of jail; nagged about his inability to keep a job, nagged about his drinking. And when the divorce was finalized, the fucking whore couldn't go two days without jumping on a new cock.

The rage boiled up to his brain and Speck saw nothing in the bar around him but technicolor spots. He forced the rage down, though. He wasn't ready yet. Wasn't ready to make Shirley pay. He wanted the anticipation to build more, so he could truly savor the moment when he knocks on her door and re-introduces himself. He turns to Elie Mae—who will be standing in for Shirley this afternoon—smiles, and orders another round, casually fingering the switchblade in his pocket.

Shortly after 10:00 that night, Speck leaves his room at the Shipyard, unfulfilled by the afternoon. Elie Mae has been unsatisfactory. He did get the tingle when he flicked open the switchblade, when he looked deep into her eyes to savor the surge of fear there, but it was cheeseclothed by the memories of her earlier giggling, of the hand on his thigh, of the whispered innuendoes. During the shared drinks, she had probably been hoping he'd take her back to his room, so now as he reflected back on his forcing her there, on what he did to her there, the issue of will is too murky for his taste.

Not like with Mrs. Harris back in April. Or when he beat the life out of that whore barmaid from Frank's Place. Or the three girls in Indiana a few weeks ago. Or those other girls in Michigan. There was no such murkiness those times. Who wielded the power then was quite clear. And it was that very clarity that Speck needed tonight.

He closes the door to his room at the Shipyard Inn and begins to walk. Towards the National Maritime Union building, where he's been hanging around the past few days, futilely waiting for a job assignment, where he knows one block east there are five two-story brick townhouses, three of them dormitories for student nurses. In the one he prefers, eight students live. Eight potential Shirleys.

Shortly after 11:00, Corazon Amurao answers a knock on the door. The man at the door is handsome, despite his dead hazel eyes. Corazon assumes, despite the late hour, that one of her roommates has a date, and turns her head to call into the rooms behind her. When she turns back, there is a third eye, the barrel of a .22 Röhm handgun, taken from Elie Mae's purse after Speck was done with her. She had mail-ordered the gun months ago. For protection.

A few minutes later, Speck has Amurao and five of her dormmates tied up with torn bedsheets. When Gloria Davy returns from a date at 11:30, she joins them. The final two roommates are bound a short while later when they also return home.

Then Richard Speck begins to play. First Suzanne Faris, then Mary Ann Jordan, Pamela Wilkening. Slicing and stabbing. Carving. Thanksgiving turkeys and Easter hams. Feeding the beast inside. But the beast is insatiable.

Nina Schmale, Patricia Matusek, Valentina Pasion, Merlita Gargullo. And still the beast rages. When Speck is no longer satisfied with the stabbing, the carving, he strangles them, a nice change of pace. When that, in turn, gets old, when his interest begins to flag, when he finds himself, as he did hours earlier after Elie Mae Hooper, unfulfilled, he rapes Gloria Davy, the night's final victim. By the end, he is exhausted and exhilarated. He basks in a post-coital glow. In the earliest hours of July 14, he heads home.

In the twenty-four years Speck would spend in prison before he dies of heart-failure, Gloria Davy was the memory that would always make him smile. It was a nice touch, he always thought. A perfect climax to the evening. And he would then chuckle at his joke. Because of all the things Richard Speck believed about himself, he was most proud of his sense of humor.

On July 14, 1966, following another night of violence and destruction, the Division St Riots simmer out.

The Chicago Cubs lose once again. Pirates pitcher Bob Veale blows through the hapless Cubbies in just over two hours, relying mostly on fastballs, with change-ups blended in as a nice change of pace. The few curveballs he throws were a nice touch. After the game, Cubs manager Lou Durocher is quoted as saying "it's just baseball."

A little more than twelve hours before Veale throws his first pitch, Corazon Amurao, unaccountably forgotten by Speck after she crawled under a bed, sticks her head out of a bedroom window and screams into Chicago, "They're all dead," her cries echoing off the brickfaces of the surrounding buildings.

Later on the 14th, Tommy John pitches a complete game for the White Sox, a 2-1 win over the Cleveland Indians, a performance White Sox manager Eddie Stanky called "quite satisfactory."

10

Somewhere on the Kittatinny Ridge, warblers flit in and out of birch and pine near an open cliff face, flashes of deep blue, black, and white peppering tree and shrub. To the warblers, there *is* no cliff face, the conception a completely alien one. Just an irrelevant absence of tree and ground. The birds are lithesome, foraging for caterpillar, crane fly, and spider, only tangentially concerned with terrestrial matters.

A doe crests what was once a path, now barely a game trail. Her hooves click and scrape rock. She is skittish, tentative; her tail swaying in anticipatory warning. Her ears are angled back, targeting a disturbance lower down the trail. A few moments of consideration and she bolts, a world entire, habitat encompassing habitat, the numerous ticks embedded in her flesh are fulsome, swollen, and legion, the *Lyme borreliosis* many carry, vectored and patient, zoonotic. All, carried away in a boundless fear bound.

The doe's exit exasperates a high-pine-branched squirrel. Tail twitching in annoyance, it barks out its complaint. The intrusion of the hiker into this perfect world does not stifle the squirrel's braggadocio, the grumbling seamlessly transferred to this newest provocation.

The ridge itself is magnificent in its unconcern. Named "Kittatinny" by the Lenni-Lenape. "Endless Mountain." Although of course it was named millennia before that. Before the mosasaur, before the trilobite. It will tolerate the hiker as it tolerates the *borreliosis*. He has stood here before, gazing at the riparian rolls of boulders below, rolling as far as he can see, the discarded agates of fickle child-gods. He has mapped his course, is cognizant of hydration and snakes, wears high-topped boots, steps knowingly, and understands the carrion-birds vectoring below would find him long before anyone else. He has stood here before; he has stood here always; within a bubble of peace of his own making, his own little world, breathing in wisdom he thinks he understands, a sentinel of nothing to no one.

He does not hear the echoes of the mountain, their whispers of dangers older than snakes, their whispers of folly, nor does he hear the echoes of profound laughter enfolded within the rock and the dirt.

A Dirge for Griffin Morris

There was really nothing about the note itself to make Griffin Morris's stomach drop. Just a hastily-scrawled message in pencil from Principal Thornton asking Griffin to come see him after fifth period. Nevertheless, when Griffin read the Post-It, he felt hollow. There was menace behind the purple square, something lurking, looming. He distractedly led band rehearsal, letting Carla Renfro's squeaky flatulence on the flute go unreproved. He didn't even have it in him to terrorize Danny Jernigans for being a full beat off the rest of the band. When it was over, he just mumbled, "Good work today, class," and ignored the puzzled stares the students cautiously shot his way as they filed out of the classroom.

When the last student left, he opened his desk drawer and took out a small vial. He shook it gently and held it up to the light. The last of the Miles Davis. After it was gone, all he'd have left at home was the Louis Armstrong, and after that, just the Baker and a handful of contemporaries.

Opening the vial tenderly, lovingly, Griffin drank off half of the cloudy liquid and replaced the vial in the drawer.

He sat quietly for a few minutes, letting the warmth flow through him. Calming, embracing, nurturing warmth. Strength, courage flowing through his timid, defeated veins.

"Maybe he wants to congratulate me on the concert," Griffin said to the empty band room.

But the moment he said it, he knew that was just the Miles Davis talking. He knew better. The band leader was always near the bottom of the pecking order at most schools, just a few notches above the janitor and a nose ahead of the art teacher. High school band leaders do not get congratulations. At best, they got tolerance. Plus, the concert had been a disaster. An unmitigated fuck-all. And even though to the best of Griffin's knowledge Thornton had never been to a single concert, he couldn't shake the suspicion that that was what the note was about.

Griffin sighed and reached back into the drawer. Even though he knew it would be next to impossible to get any more Miles, he polished off what was in the vial. As a second dose of warmth and courage coursed through him, Griffin ducked into the boys' bathroom, took in his reflection. He did not see a middle-aged, balding, forty-pounds-overweight band teacher. He did not see the disheveled dress shirt, haphazardly tucked behind a cracked and faded belt, did not see the stained and worn jacket, the scuffed shoes. He saw Griffin Morris as he was *meant* to be. And that Griffin Morris was not going to take any shit from Principal Thornton.

He would bolt right past Marcy, that twisted old crone of a secretary, and storm right into Thornton's office.

"Let's get something straight, Curtis," Griffin would say before Thornton could begin, knowing he'd bristle at Griffin's decorum-breaching use of his first name, "I've had enough of this school's half-assed support of me and my music program. This school is damn lucky to have someone with my reputation, with my talent. I *condescend* to be here, Curtis. Do you understand that? I condescend. But that condescension has a price. The music program's budget needs to be doubled. And I need a new auditorium. A tin can has better acoustics than that cavern I'm forced to use now."

He would rail; he would demand; he would threaten and intimidate. He would insist and, he knew as the Miles Davis reached its zenith, he would receive.

Griffin blew past Marcy, as in the vision, and entered the inner office. Thornton sat behind a massive mahogany desk. The desk, his van dyke, and his navy-blue serge suit made him look more like a robber-baron than a school administrator. Like he should be spending his time busting unions. It was a cultivated look that Griffin despised.

"Let's get something straight, Curt—"

"Cut the pleasantries, Morris, and sit down."

Thornton bored through Griffin with cold, challenging eyes. Griffin tried to hold the gaze, to stare him back down, but after a few moments of awkward silence, he looked away. His eyes flicked up to the paddle mounted on the wall behind Thornton. An antiquated relic from days long gone by and, Griffin had no doubt, achingly missed.

"What in *God's name* was that?" Thornton asked after his crafted lingering pause.

"What was what?"

"That sad-sack cacophony you called a Spring Concert."

"I thought the kids did a good job," Griffin lied.

"It was an abomination. Like two cats fucking in a blender. Seriously, Griffin," Thornton said in a somewhat softer tone, "what are you teaching these kids? How is it the concerts get worse and worse each year?"

"I didn't know you came to them."

"I don't. Not until last night, anyway. But I heard things. Like that *you* play *your* trumpet with the band. Wouldn't have believed it if I hadn't seen it with my own eyes. What is *that* about, Morris? Conductors are supposed to have those little stick thingies, not play with the damn band like some goddamned regressive.

"We don't have anyone who can play first trumpet."

"What you *have* is a group of kids who, for some damn reason, are interested in music, who *want* to play, who want to *learn*. Yet, you can't teach them. And twice a year, you put your lack of ability on public display. You humiliate the kids, you humiliate their parents, you humiliate this school, and you humiliate yourself. All so you can play your horn? And the playlist you chose? Really? You think these kids can handle Mozart? Gershwin? Stick to 'Hot-Cross Buns' and 'Skip to My Lou.'"

The Miles-courage bled-dry, Griffin mumbled, "Was there any part of it you enjoyed?"

"Yeah," Thornton said. "When it was over."

Griffin sat at his particle-board desk, pouring Franzia Cab Sav into a red Solo cup. The only light in the room the electric glow of the laptop screen as he waited for Chaucon to respond to his panicked email. In hindsight, he regretted the rashness of polishing off the rest of the Miles Davis this afternoon and knew he would pay a pretty penny to get more. If he even *could* get more.

While he waited, he fiddled with the dwindling stock assembled in front of him. Two vials of Wynton Marsalis, a vial of Herb Alpert, a couple each of Terence Blanchard and Arturo Sandoval, one Chet Baker, and then his remaining crown jewel—the Louis Armstrong. Being saved for a truly special occasion. Fingering the vial, the cloudy liquid coy and flirtatious, Griffin's thoughts drifted toward Thaddeus.

Thad was the student every high school band leader dreams about. His depth of musical knowledge was encyclopedic. His enthusiasm unchecked. His innovation chastised Griffin daily, a cosmic rebuke, a reprimand for his own abandoned potential.

And the music! The way Thad wielded that trombone! Splendor not heard since J.J. Johnson. Listening to Thad, your body became enfolded, embraced by liquid brass. A warmth coursed through your body and you sensed the closest approximation of God. Or at least, that's how Griffin thought of it.

And then someone mentioned Julliard to his parents. And off he went. And that year's Spring Concert, one in which he felt bold enough to include "Ode to Joy," was left to the gaggle of untalented dregs Thad left behind. It did not go well.

And then a few years later, Marcus Jones appeared. The way that kid could bang a drum! Could rip out a solo electric, make you feel thunder in your soul. And the kid was smart, too. Knew his music. Understood Ringo was the most important Beatle. And Marcus brought that same essential pacing to the school band. A completely different species than hacks like Danny Jernigans.

But Griffin fucked that one up. He winced at the memory, made a reflexive reach for one of the vials before checking himself. No one could blame him for losing Thaddeus to Julliard. But Marcus? Marcus was all on him.

He tried to get too close. Pushed too hard. Offered him private lessons after school. Held him to a higher standard than the other students. Made it clear he had greater expectations for Marcus.

Marcus held out for a little more than a month. Then he started to come to band practice late. Then he started not coming at all. And then one day he told Griffin he was quitting. Had an offer to join a band, he said. A *rock* band! Low-hanging fruit. Like Buddy Rich says, "If you don't have ability, you wind up playing in a rock band." Marcus *had* ability, dammit! But there was a record deal, and all that came with rock bands and record deals. How could Griffin compete with that?

The fact the band has enjoyed a modest, steady notoriety, that Marcus chased a dream (compromised though it may be) and caught it, did little to soften the stab of loss Griffin felt every time their songs played on the radio.

A ping broke into Griffin's thoughts.

Chaucon had replied: "I can get you two vials. $400 each."

"Jesus Christ!" Griffin exclaimed out loud. "Eight hundred! Is he out of his mind?"

His emailed reply asked as much. While he awaited the reply to his reply, he glanced around the room. The only furnishings beyond the desk were a tattered sleeper he moved in when he decided to convert his bedroom into a studio for private lessons, an IKEA coffee table, a matching end table holding his turntable, and a small, two-shelf bookcase for his vinyl. From the walls, puttied posters of Dizzy Gillespie, Buddy Bolden, and the great Satchmo himself stared down.

Griffin found their stares disapproving, judgmental. They, the glares seemed to proclaim, would not suffer Thornton. Would not let themselves be talked to that way. Would not let Thornton pivot from humiliation to thinly-veiled threat.

"Enough small talk," Thornton said. "Let's get to the point."

The humiliation, Griffin assumed, *was* the point.

"I've been asked to recommend a series of budget cuts for the next school year. And while I have always held that a school band is important, I'm not sure a dedicated band *teacher* is. After last night, I'm much less sure."

"You're going to replace me?"

"We'd eliminate the position entirely, so it wouldn't look like a reflection on you." Which, of course, it was. "Gladys could take over the band."

"Gladys! You've got to be kidding me! She couldn't tell the difference between a half note and a good, solid, meat fart."

"Yes, well, she's been the music teacher here for more than twenty years. And she's safe. She'll put on concerts with '*Frère Jacques*' and 'Camptown Races,' parents will fall asleep, wake up in time to clap for their kids, go home and forget the concert ever happened. No Mozart, no fucking Beethoven. Just simple shit kids can play. Everything will stay smooth. And safe."

"You mean boring."

"I mean smooth. And safe."

After a few moments of strained silence, in which Griffin sagged in the chair, defeat tickling him inside, Thornton softened his tone again.

"I like to consider myself a fair man, Morris. You've put in twelve years of service here, no matter the quality of that service. Look, I know this is not where you thought you'd end up. You had bigger dreams, grander plans. You think this is all beneath you. Shake out of it, son. Stop chasing your tail. There is no shame in any of this. There's nobility here. And you could find it, if you deigned to look.

"I don't have to make a final decision just yet. I can hold off for a while. Until after the Winter Concert, say. Give you a shot at changing my mind. But let me be clear, Morris. Angels better sing. I shit you not. Angels better descend from the fucking heavens and fill my ears with honey and ambrosia."

And now Griffin sat in a darkened room, wondering where to find honey and ambrosia when another ping interrupted his thoughts.

Chaucon again:

"*Mon frère*, there's an extremely limited supply. Miles is not exactly around to keep filling those spit valves. You want the vials or not?"

Griffin did. And even though eight hundred dollars was almost half his monthly salary, even though he sometimes suspects that French Canadian bastard is laughing at him, sitting up there in his Montreal club, splashing dish soap into water and calling it Miles Davis, he knew he would pay it. Because he needed that connection, that affirmation, the recognition of a could-be colleague.

He sent his reply and then glanced up at the great Satchmo again. The look on Louis's face as he blazed that brass. Pure bliss. Like the angelic host was calling him home. At the end of a long, shitty day, Griffin smiled. Grabbed his trumpet off the coffee table, uncorked a vial of Marsalis, and went into the studio. He knew he would never get to the place captured in that poster but tonight, as he felt the first tingles of that warm affirmation touch his fingers, he'd try to get as close to it as he could.

There was a time when Griffin could get pretty damn close to that place.

He found his grandfather's bugle when he was eight, and from the moment he began to parrot his grandfather, mastering "Reveille" and "Taps," it was clear he had a gift. In high school, people began using the word "prodigy." The only reason Julliard was never mentioned was because no one in the small town of Altamont, Kansas, knew such a place existed. But KU came calling. Offering a full scholarship to be part of the Marching Jayhawks.

And his trumpet won over Becky Sanderson. He stood outside her house, played "Sea of Love" and "In Your Eyes," and then when he asked, she said she'd go to the prom with him instead of Mack Bulger, the all-state linebacker who everyone knew was sweet on her.

On the afternoon of the prom, as Griffin was driving into Parsons to pick up a corsage for Becky, flashing blue and red lights filled the rearview mirror. A few moments later, Sheriff Bulger's fetid coffee breath filled the car.

"Well, well, well, if it isn't the Morris kid? Where you headed off to in such a hurry, son?"

"I wasn't speeding."

"'I wasn't speeding, sir.'"

"Sorry, Sheriff. I wasn't speeding, sir."

"Do you know what the speed limit on this road is, son?"

"Fifty-five miles per hour."

Sheriff Bulger stood erect, looked over Griffin's car at the deputy that had sidled up to the passenger side window.

"Looks like we got ourselves a bit of an attitude-problem here." The cheap coffee cloud with a faint hint of near-expired cream was back at the car window. "Fifty-five miles an hour, *sir.*'"

"Yes, sir. Sorry, Sheriff."

"Not yet, you're not. Well, I clocked you at seventy."

"There's no way!" Griffin blurted out despite himself. He doubted his rusted-out truck could even reach that speed.

Sheriff Bulger stood up again. Again, spoke over the car. "See what I mean about an attitude-problem, Wilson?"

"I sure do, Sheriff."

Bulger leaned into the window. Inhaled deeply. "Say, Deputy Wilson? Do you detect a distinct odor emanating from this vehicle?" A wry, Cheshire-Cat smile.

"Why yes I do, Sheriff."

"Seems like the Morris boy here is a bourbon man."

"Seems that way, Sheriff."

"I haven't been drinking."

Sheriff Bulger raised an interrogative eyebrow.

"Sir," Griffin added.

"All the same, I suppose for the safety of all the other drivers in Labette County, we might should just haul you in. To be on the safe side."

Four hours later, Griffin was still in the holding cell, powerless and gelded.

"Hey there, Loverboy."

The words broke into Griffin's despair. Sheriff Bulger stood before the gate, a Colossus in serge. He smirked at Griffin, tapping his watch with a finger.

"Didn't your prom start half an hour ago?" A mocking sad face. "I don't think you're going to make it. Sorry about that, son. But don't you worry about that Sanderson girl. My boy will be sure and show her a good time."

Griffin leaped to his feet, grabbing the bars. "What the hell is wrong with you people?"

At the sign of aggression, paltry though it was, Deputy Wilson and a second deputy entered the holding area.

"Everything ok, boss?" Deputy Wilson asked.

"Oh, sure. Everything's just fine. The Morris boy here was just askin' if we could teach him a bit about manners. And about respecting the duly elected authority of Labette County. And I was just a sayin' 'why, sure. That can be arranged.'"

The baton was rattlesnake fast. Just a black blur. Followed by a broken time riff of ringing metal and crunching bone.

"Damn! You hear that crunch, Wilson? I'd say something sure as hell broke in there. Couple a' fingers at least. Maybe the whole hand. And that's a damn shame. I heard tell you got a scholarship 'cause you play that trumpet so pretty. Could be hard to play, I imagine, with a broken hand."

"You're done," Griffin said, clutching his hand, believing the lie true. "My parents will sue. They'll have you fired."

The sheriff's smile deepened, etched to chiseled. He chuckled, looked over at Deputy Wilson and winked.

"Well, I suppose you are right about that. Word gets out we broke your hand, we would have some explaining to do. Of course, when we tell about how you were drunk, became combative, assaulted Deputy Wilson here, well shoot, I don't think they'll be much of a stink. People will shake their heads, say 'boys will be boys,' note that it sure is a shame what happened to your hand, and carry on with whatever they was doing. Ain't that about the size of it, Deputy Wilson?"

"Sounds about right."

"Anything you care to add, Deputy Grunder?"

"No, Sheriff, I think that's about the size of it."

The smile erased. "But of course, you're gonna keep that mouth of yours shut."

"Why the hell would I do that?"

The chuckle again. "Oh, we can be pretty persuasive on that score when we have a mind."

To Deputy Wilson: "I believe the boy had that trumpet of his in his truck?"

"Yes, sir, he did."

"Go get it. And grab the Polaroid from the storage cabinet. We want to be sure and document this evening."

Sheriff Bulger opened a desk drawer and pulled out a latex glove, snapped it on. He reached back in and pulled out a jar of Vaseline.

"We're gonna see just how talented you are, boy. We're gonna see if that big mouth of yours ain't the only hole you can play your horn on."

He leaned in close to Griffin's face, fetid coffee-breath once again suffocating him. The chuckle and the Cheshire-Cat smile.

"That Sanderson girl ain't the only one gonna get fucked tonight."

After that night, it would take years before Griffin could bring himself to touch an instrument, any instrument, again. He came back to it gradually. Finding his way back to the bugle first. "Taps," then "Reveille." Eventually, he made tentative essays on other brass. Cornet. Flugel Horn. Trombone. But even two decades after Sherriff Bulger, Griffin still could not bring himself to touch a trumpet.

He knew during all the intervening time that this wasn't right. That if they could, Louis and Buddy and Dizzy would scream down at him from the walls:

"Play! Just play! Pick up that trumpet and blow! Didn't you learn anything listening to us? You don't get *over* it; you get *through* it. You play your damn way through sorrow. You cram all of your grief as tightly as you can into that diaphragm of yours and you make that grief sing. You don't wait for it to scab over. You pick at it. Keep it fresh, keep it raw. And you make it into beauty. Just what the hell do you think jazz is all about, son? It's about coming through slaughter. And it ain't just jazz, as you damn well know. Beethoven went deaf, turned that shit into 'Ode to Joy.' So, pick yourself up and play! Just play!"

Griffin knew this. Knew all of it. But none of it made picking up the trumpet possible. He'd try, and try, and try, and just couldn't do it. Until one day he could.

But even then, once he allowed himself to dance those valves again, he was just chasing. Chasing what the music promised. Chasing the last pure breath of oxygen in an atmosphere of stale, suffocating fog. Just that, and nothing more.

This wasn't the right way either.

He knew the kids made fun of what they saw as an overblown intensity. He knew that parents found his grabbing the moment during school concerts, playing alongside their children instead of leading them, strange, uncomfortable. And Griffin knew what drove his obsessive interest in Thaddeus and later Marcus, knew that he was using them, chasing vicariously.

But knowing was a far cry from stopping. Knowing just gave the hurt depth and echo. So Griffin stuffed the knowing inside, ignored it, projected magical powers of communion onto vials of spit, and under cover of high-school cacophony or in the solitude of his own studio, tried to play his way through.

And now Thornton was threatening to take even *that* away from him.

At the first full band practice of the new school year, when Wilson Parker shuffled in the stylized coolness of his bright yellow Chuck Taylor's to an open chair in the brass section, unpacked a dull, finger-smudged trumpet and began to play, Griffin knew exactly what this was, what was being offered him. Wilson Parker was a gift. An opportunity. The Universe, in its random indifference, had just tossed a life raft to the speck It had been casually trying to drown. Into each and every song the band practiced that day, Parker wove into the air the very honey and ambrosia Thornton demanded last spring. The very honey and ambrosia.

Griffin was giddy that night. He washed down dinner with one of the new vials of Miles and then the Baker. An impulsive overindulgence. And rash, he knew. But the excitement was too real. Had to be acknowledged somehow. He'd been given another chance.

Griffin did not sleep that night. He just played, and planned, and dreamed. Of liquid brass. Of honey and ambrosia. And of applause.

He pushed Wilson all September and the kid ate it up. No matter what Griffin threw at him, either in the full band sessions or in the once-a-week, fifteen-minute, one-on-one sessions Griffin held with each band student, Wilson absorbed it. The music became his exhale. And the genre didn't matter. Parker could handle Sousa and Gershwin with the same panache with which he dispatched Stephen Foster.

And each night, Griffin fantasized a Winter program of exalted ambition. He dreamed of the braggadocious force of Chicago's "25 or 6 to 4." Perhaps something bold and zesty, some Cab Calloway. Something trendy? "Seven Nation Army"? For the purists, he'd toss in some Glenn Miller, and then, a crescendo. Maybe John Williams. The theme from *Star Wars*. It'd be a Winter Concert no one would forget. Thornton could choke on it. And Wilson was only a freshman. Griffin would have him for four years! Four years of Spring and Winter Concerts of such magnificence, such glory, that the only word listeners would use would be "transcendent." Parker would be celebrated. And Griffin? He would be recognized at long last. Acclaimed. Completed.

He fully understood the rest of the kids would struggle with that material. They weren't up to it. But, his fervor argued, this is what they all *really* wanted anyway. Those kids didn't want '*Frère Jacques*' and 'Camptown Races.' They wanted music that was fun. That challenged them. That made them feel they were playing *actual* music, not sleepwalking through someone else's echoes. Sometimes, late at night, when he thought of Danny Jernigans, Carla Renfro, and the others waddling their discordant way through "Minnie the Moocher" he almost gave up the dream. But then he'd sip on some of the Herb Alpert or the Blanchard and remind himself: Wilson Parker will be there to lead them. And *he* would be there to lead Wilson Parker.

***

"Can you all hear how Wilson attacks that bridge?"

"You gotta French-kiss that note, like Wilson does."

"Danny, you are so far behind Wilson you're in front of him."

At first, Wilson seemed to enjoy the attention. Met it with a blend of innocent wonder and justified confidence. But as the praise grew more effusive, Wilson seemed to grow more uncomfortable.

Griffin was slow to recognize the signs. He thought it all a product of modesty, which made him adore Wilson all the more. So humble. So unassuming. There would be no losing Wilson to Juilliard or to some glorified garage band.

Griffin pushed harder, became less and less subtle about his favoritism. Made Wilson First Chair. Installed two separate solos for him in the program. Offered Wilson the mouthpiece from his own trumpet when he suspected the boy's was too shallow. The flashes of discomfort Griffin chalked up to pressure. Pressure, he reasoned, was good. Pressure inspired great music. Pressure, Griffin thought at night as he sipped a Sandoval, makes diamonds.

"Can I talk to you for a few seconds, Mr. Morris?"

"Absolutely, Wilson. And, please, call me Griffin. What can I do for you? Is that mouthpiece not working out?"

"No, sir. It's fine. It's not that."

"OK."

"It's about the solos."

"What about them?"

"Do we have to have two of them?"

"I think solos are the best way to showcase your talent."

"Yes, sir. But I've been thinking about it. I really don't want to do two. Not sure I want to do any, but I certainly don't want two."

There was a hint of firmness to this. The suggestion of a foot down. A coldness gripped Griffin. His fingers slowly crawled towards his desk drawer. Who'd he bring today? Avishai Cohen? The last of the Marsalis? The Thomas Marriot that Chaucon had BOGOed him because no one bought Marriot anymore?

"OK, Wilson. We'll just do the one solo. The first one. Anything else?"

"Yes, sir. That first solo."

"Yes?"

"Does it have to be 'When the Saints Go Marching In'?"

"What's wrong with 'When the Saints Go Marching In'? It's one of the great Louis Armstrong songs."

"Yeah, but . . . ."

"Yes? But?"

"Well, I'm not Louis Armstrong."

"Not yet. But you've got that kind of talent. I see that. And that kind of talent should be showcased."

Wilson did not look convinced or comfortable.

"I'll tell you what," Griffin pressed on. "I've got time between now and the concert to work with you. Private lessons, free of charge, after school every day for an hour. No, no, no, it'll be my pleasure. We'll work on that solo until you're whistling it in your sleep. How's that sound?"

"I don't know if I can do that, Mr. Morris. I have baseball practice most days."

"Baseball?" Griffin spit the word out like it was a moldy strawberry. "A talent like yours shouldn't be playing baseball. What if you hurt your fingers? Break your hand? Why would you risk everything playing baseball?"

After a pensive pause: "Because it's fun."

"And isn't this fun?" Griffin asked.

Again, the pause: "Sometimes."

He knew the right thing, the proper thing to do was to scale the program back. Take the pressure off of Wilson. Just let him be a kid. Find enjoyment in the trumpet. Instead, he opened the final Miles Davis vial, slammed it down, and grabbed his car keys. There was a new trumpet in the window of Lily's Music, a Bach Stradivarius.

"Go buy it for the kid," Miles Davis whispered to Griffin, "That cat kid will dig it. Dig it more than he digs baseball."

Griffin was surprisingly relaxed as he watched from behind the stage curtain as the parents filed into the auditorium.

Relaxed despite the thoroughly unpleasant conversation he had with Thornton this morning.

"Shall I consider this your letter of resignation," he asked Griffin, holding up a copy of the concert program. "Chicago? John Williams? Louis Armstrong? Ode to Joy? Are you out of your fucking mind?"

"The kids have been working really hard. I think you'll be impressed."

"Whatever. It's your funeral."

Relaxed despite the trumpet fiasco. Wilson would not accept the Stradivarius. Recoiled as if from rancid meat when Griffin offered it. No amount of pleading could convince him to take it.

"Won't I feel more comfortable playing the solo with the instrument I've been practicing with, Mr. Morris?" he said, a suggestion laced with unacknowledged threat.

A nagging fear tickled Griffin.

"But you *are* still playing the solo, right? You're still coming to the concert?" He hoped Wilson did not note the pleading tone. The sudden, gasped breathing.

There was a pause, awkward and agonizing, before Wilson replied: "Yes, sir. I'll still play."

"You promise?" the question leaped out.

"Yes. I promise."

"Swear."

"I swear."

But Wilson's chair in the brass section was empty ten minutes before the concert was to begin.

"People run late. Happens all the time. He'll be here," Chet Baker (replaced at a third of last month's pay) whispered to Griffin as he fingered a new conductor's baton, purchased when he returned the Stradivarius.

When the chair was still empty five minutes out, Griffin longed for vials he did not bring. At two minutes past, his shoulders slumped, a dog anticipating the kick, he shuffled over to his instrument case, exchanged the baton for his trumpet, and shuffled out to the podium to face the music.

It certainly wasn't the transcendent performance he'd spent the last few months dreaming of, but he had to admit the kids did as good a job as could be expected. The opening bars of the *Stars Wars* theme were carried off admirably and "Seven Nation Army" was *almost* recognizable. As for the rest, Griffin realized if the material had been more calibrated to his students' abilities, it would have been quite good. Without question, it was one of the better concerts in recent memory, and Griffin reasoned that if Thornton was inclined to be impartial, it was probably good enough to save his job.

As Griffin shuffled across the auditorium, passively absorbing reflexive congratulations from homogenous parents, he felt a pull at his sleeve. Danny Jernigans.

"How did we do, Mr. Morris?"

For a second, Griffin pushed the image of an empty chair from his mind and focused his full attention on the boy before him. He took him all in. The eager smile poorly hiding the boy's great need for validation.

"You did just fine, Danny. Just fine. And, please," he added spontaneously, "call me Griffin." He reached out and tousled the boy's hair, met the boy's quizzical look with an inscrutable smile.

Griffin held this smile as he completed the congratulatory lap around the auditorium, shaking hands, thanking parents for coming. It was still there on the drive home. Still there when the faces of Dizzy, Buddy, and Satchmo greeted him upon his return to the apartment.

For a long while, Griffin just sat at his desk. Opening its drawer, he took out the vial of Louis Armstrong, considered it.

He had a hard time identifying the feeling coursing through him. It wasn't happiness; that much he knew. Nor was it satisfaction. And it wasn't exactly peace, nor contentment, but it seemed perhaps a distant cousin of those. If he had to guess at the best word, he'd say it was recognition, but that wasn't quite it either. What he did know, with sudden questionless clarity, was that *this* was the day he'd been saving Louis for. He opened the vial and sipped slowly, with relish, savoring each brackish drop.

When it was empty, Griffin carried the empty vial to the garage and tossed it into the recycling can. He looked around the room as if he had never entered it before. He found the hose, then some duct tape. It took just a few minutes to rig. He was about to begin when a thought occurred to him, sending him back into the apartment, returning to the garage a few moments later with a CD jewel case in his hand.

As he sat in the running car, "When the Saint's Come Marching In," flowing from the speakers, he dreamed of a procession. They were all there. Dizzy, Buddy, Miles, Chet, Marsalis, and, of course, the great Satchmo. Marching down streets lined with people, wrought-iron gates adorned with the *flor-de-lis* in front of every house, they bestowed honey and ambrosia. At the front of this group, ceded a place of distinction, Griffin Morris marched and played. Satchmo patted his shoulder and smiled. Miles caught his eye and said "Cool, man. Cool."

A warmth he had longed for for years flowed through his body. Through the car windshield he could make out shadowy figures moving in squares of light. He became dimly aware of a rhythmic pounding. Panicked. Insistent. Demanding.

With his last moments of consciousness, Griffin convinced himself that these were the percussive beats of an angelic orchestra, the opening movement of a symphony, calling him home.

All-American

"there's danger on the edge of town"
    Jim Morrison

The killer awoke before dawn. He put his boots on and he walked on down the hall. His wife, Mary, was in the kitchen, working on breakfast. Eggs over-easy, bacon, and pancakes. On the table, she had already placed the milk, the OJ, and some toast, pats of butter sliding off their edges like cars forced off a cliff.

"You're up early," Mary said. "I figured you'd sleep in a bit after you got home so late."

She placed a mug of steaming coffee before him and pivoted to the stove with the grace of a ballerina. Alex watched her lithe movements and felt a tightening of desire.

"Who you working for today?" Mary's question broke into his thoughts.

"Carbone."

"Oh, honey. I don't like it when you work for Carbone. Everyone he sends you after is always packing. Or is surrounded by goons who are. It's too dangerous."

"For me, or for them?"

Mary chose to ignore that. "Why can't you do more jobs like that one for the mother who wanted her daughter to be head cheerleader? Killing high-school girls seems so much safer than going after mobsters."

"I wouldn't worry, sweetheart, I think it's a long-range job. Carbone told me to bring The Reacher."

She seemed only partially mollified by this. She leaned back against the stove, arms akimbo, and watched as he removed a double-bladed six-inch tactical stiletto from its ankle-sheath. He reached for the wet stone and oil, kept next to the salt, pepper, and sugar shakers where the table met the wall.

"I don't understand why you work for men like him."

"He pays well. Very well. Like our vacation-to-the-Bahamas-this-spring well. And Carbone and the others aren't exactly men you can say no to too many times."

"You have a family, you know."

And right on cue, Samantha skipped into the kitchen.

"Morning, Mom. Hiya, Daddy." Samantha stamped each greeting with a kiss and sat down, watching, enthralled, as her father pulled the stiletto across the stone.

"Can I do that, Daddy?"

"Well, sweetie. I think your brother could use the practice. If he ever wakes up, that is."

"Well, can I clean the gun, then?"

"Sure, sweetie."

He reached into his jacket, removed his short-barrel .357 from its shoulder holster and slid the gun across the table. "You remember where the kit is?"

She was back in a flash, mixing sips of orange juice and nibbles of toast between squirts of oil into the revolver's chambers and thrusts of the bore brush. She was fast, efficient, and effective. Pride surged as he watched her.

"Daddy?"

"What is it, sweetie?"

"Todd asked me to the dance. I'd really like to go with him. He's *so* dreamy. Can I say 'yes'? Please, Daddy?"

He glanced over at Mary and saw his own thoughts reflected. Samantha was only fifteen. A freshman. Was it safe to let her start dating? And Todd was a junior, wasn't he? He remembered when he was a junior. The peer pressure, the tall tales, the race to be first, how he and his friends saw the freshmen girls as lambs to be led. He would sure hate to have to put a bullet in Todd. Or worse. Make it last longer—a lot longer, perhaps—if he felt the situation warranted.

"Your mother and I will have to talk about that."

"Can you let me know soon? I'm afraid he'll ask someone else if I wait too long."

"Sure, sweetie. We'll let you know tonight, after I get back from work."

"Who are you killing today, Daddy?"

"I don't know yet. Have to go meet Mr. Carbone here in a few. That reminds me, can you go get The Reacher for me? I'll need it today."

"Sure thing, Daddy." She bounded out of the kitchen; but before he and Mary could touch on the subject of her dating Todd or anyone else, Ricky shuffled into the kitchen.

"Morning, Son."

"Morning, honey."

"Hey."

"Want to finish sharpening the knife?" he asked.

The question like a cup of coffee, Ricky immediately perked up. "Seriously?"

"Sure. You remember how?"

"Yes sir, 45-degree angle, circular pulls."

"That's right. You're doing fine, son. Just like that."

And again, he felt the pride surge. Such good kids.

"Hey, Dad," Ricky said in between passes, "I was wondering if you'd reconsider letting me get *Call of Duty* for the Xbox. I've got the money for it; been saving up my allowance and everything. Please?"

He exchanged another reflected look with Mary.

"Oh, I don't know," Mary said. "I'm not a fan of those first-person shooter games. So sensational."

"Oh, c'mon, Mom!"

"No, son. Your mother's right. That game's far too violent for someone your age.

"Or any age," Mary mumbled as she set Ricky's breakfast in front of him.

"Oh, man. I never get to do anything."

"Well, now, son, hold on there. That's not fair. When the Carleys got that dog, kept barking all night, remember? Your mother couldn't get a good night's sleep for weeks. Who'd we let take care of that? Not too many thirteen-year-olds get to make to make ground beef and arsenic patties."

Ricky smiled.

"Yeah. That goddamned dog tore his own guts out trying to stop the pain."

"Language!" Mary scolded.

"Sorry, Mom."

"And Bring-Your-Child-to-Work Day is coming right up."

"Really!?! You mean it, I can come this year?"

"Lucky Dog," Samantha said as she re-entered the kitchen carrying the rifle case. "You're gonna have a blast." She then snorted at her unintentional joke.

Looking at his daughter holding the case, he got lost in reverie, memories of last year. How adept she had been at tracking the target, the calmness with which she pulled the trigger, the serenity afterwards. She was a natural. He deposited the entire fee into her college-fund in recognition.

"How was work last night, Daddy?" Samantha's question brought him back to the kitchen.

"Oh, piece of cake. Some stuffed-shirt uptown lawyer, working the lawsuit against Senator Griggs."

"Oh, I've been following that story online," Mary said. "So interesting."

"Well," he said, laughing. "It's gonna be a lot more interesting now."

His family laughed with him.

"So," Samantha said once the laughter died down. "What'd you use?"

Nodding in Ricky's direction, he answered, "The stiletto. I tell you, his neck was flapping like a Muppet's mouth."

Once again, his family laughed with him. He looked at his watch.

"I better get going. Carbone gets a little grumpy if he's kept waiting."

The revolver and stiletto re-housed, The Reacher in its case in his hand, he did a circuit of good-bye kisses.

"Bye, Dad."

"I love you, Daddy."

"Have a good day at work, honey."

Pausing a moment on the front porch, he took in the morning in all its splendor. The sun shining, bright and warm; a dove perched on a power line, cooing a morning benediction. He filled his lungs deep, and smiled. Yes, it was going to be a blessed day.

Like all the days before it and all the days still to come.

Here Be Monsters

The world was all before him. Or that's how it seemed to Miles, standing at the edge of the old woman's back yard, vast, fulsome, and green. He filled his lungs with the foreign smell of fresh-cut grass, laced with just a fecund hint of manure from an unseen farm, and smiled. An adventure lay before him. The verdant acreage seemingly unlimited. Cutting across the back quarter, a gently-rolling creek, its singing susurrus a lullaby. And, if he could figure a way to cross the creek without getting his new Skechers with the flashing LED lights he had begged his mom for months to buy wet, there was the woods beyond. And beyond that? Who knew? At the edges of the maps of the old explorers, the ones whose names were invocations to Miles—de Soto, de Gama, Magellan, Pizarro—were labeled with admonitions and warnings: Here Be Monsters; or, Here Be Dragons when they wished to be more precise. How Miles loved to read of these men, these conquering heroes, in his World Book Children's Encyclopedia, how he internalized the rhyme, "In the year 1492, Columbus sailed the ocean blue" as if it was an incantation, how he longed to find a world of his own, unexplored and far away. And here it was. Vast, fulsome, and green.

Miles once again breathes deep and smiles. He takes his first steps toward the creek, and beyond the creek, the woods, and beyond that? Who knew? The world was all before him. Where to choose?

"We're going to have a little adventure, you and I," his mother said the night before, hastily throwing clothes into his roller suitcase, the one emblazoned with Buzz Lightyear and his bravado catch phrase: "To Infinity, and Beyond." She was packing like it was a game, like she was trying to beat a specific time. Chasing a record.

In the rush of excitement and novelty, Miles failed to notice things, small details, details that his nine-year-old brain wouldn't understand, but which would be stored in memory, parsed over, analyzed from the wizened perspective of Miles-as-adult, details like his mom's shaking hands, her subtle movements to keep the left side of her face from view. Miles-the-child failed to notice these things. Instead, Miles-the-child asked,

"Is Daddy coming?"

"No," his mother answered, perhaps a bit too quickly (although this too, Miles-the-child missed). "Your Daddy is not coming with us. This adventure is just for you and me."

And for some unexamined reason, this satisfied Miles. And so, he helped his mother pack, helped her beat that specific time she seemed to be chasing.

They drove through the dark night, down back roads, his mother marking the occasion as special with a stop at a roadside convenience store, buying Miles a candy bar and a chocolate milk. Miles chewed the Snicker's bar, drank the milk, slowly, savoringly, honoring the rareness of it. Then, despite the sugar rush, despite the novelty of the night, Miles fell asleep, his head pressed to the car door window, against which the reflection of headlights against the roadside reflectors were reflected back.

When Miles awoke, it was day again. Had been for a few hours. The car was parked beside a large blue house fading to gray, the color of a fading bruise. His mother gave Miles a shakily-propped smile, a look that seemed laden with import beyond him.

"Here we are," she said, in a voice that seemed hollow, emptied of certainty.

The old woman, in a denim dress broken only by a white strip of cloth used as a belt, let them in, gestured them into what she called "her parlor," offered Miles gumdrops from a crystal bowl.

"I know it's early," she said to his mother, "but after all."

Miles was disappointed to find that no matter the color of the gumdrop, it was licorice-flavored, the flavor of staleness; like the old woman's dress, of a by-gone era, a taste faintly reminiscent of dust.

There was talk of paperwork. The old woman said "and of course, we don't use real names here." His mother spoke with the caught-breath of holding something in, something back. There were periods of silence. After one of these, the old woman suggested Miles go outside, explore the back yard.

Before the door closed, the old woman added an admonition to be careful near the creek.

But that's where Miles eventually found himself. At first, he just ran around in the vast greenness of the lawn, luxuriating in its vastness, its greenness, things Miles had only dreamed about, things so novel, so foreign.

But then, Miles was at the creek. Not for the sake of the creek, but for what lay beyond. He was old enough to know there were no elves in the woods beyond, but still young enough to regret this knowledge. There would be animals in there, though. Animals that, if he was quiet, and patient, he might see. The wildest animal he ever saw at home was an over-urbanized squirrel racing across the chain-link fence surrounding the dust-choked rectangle back lot behind the townhouse that until yesterday . . .

But who knew what wonders he could see in these woods? Deer, certainly; maybe a porcupine, or even a hippogriff.

No! he chided himself for his foolish, childish forgetfulness. *Not a hippogriff. There are no such things.*

So, not a hippogriff, but maybe, Miles thought in a spirit of mollification, maybe a leopard.

Miles stood at the water's edge, worrying about how to cross. How would Pizzaro or Balboa or de Leon handle such an obstacle? But before Miles's imagination could retrofit the facts and figures from his encyclopedia into an answer, something caught his eye. Something metal, blinking in the morning sun.

An old fishing net, rust-mottled, artificial-green nylon webbing mostly frayed. Mostly. There was still enough netting intact to encourage Miles to grab the handle, dip the webbing into the creek, and run along its shore. At first, he was unsure if he'd catch anything. Then, with the stubborn, recidivist optimism of youth, he was unsure what he'd catch. A frog, maybe, or a fish. Maybe a whale. *Yes. That was it*, Miles thought to himself. *I'll catch a whale.* The unacknowledged impossibility of such a thought made him run a little faster.

Miles ran. He ran as if he was trying to beat a specific time. He ran as if chasing a record. He ran until he was out of breath, and could run no more. Then he pulled out the net to see what he caught.

Miles did not catch a frog. Nor was there a fish in his net, unexpectedly thrust into an intolerable, unsustainable environment and gasping for breath. And Miles most certainly did not catch a whale.

But he did catch something. There, tangled in the mostly-frayed artificial green netting, was a monster.

Armored and clawed, the faded red of a scabbed-over wound. Eight spindly legs writhed, as if a second creature was trapped underneath, desperate to flee. Its two unearthly eyes stared up at Miles, giving nothing back. Two antennae, protruding just above the creature's churning mandibles (a word Miles had only a theoretical knowledge of via his World Book Children's Encyclopedia), waved wildly like a demented conductor's baton, or a switch cut to fit a punishment. To either side of these, over-sized claws flapped and clapped in dreadful applause.

Miles's thoughts—if thoughts they could be called enmeshed in such horror—were of parasitic blood-drinkers, of demons and devils, of the warnings and admonitions scrawled onto the edges of maps. He drops the net as if stung. As it floats down the creek with its monstrous rider, Miles runs back to the house. He is desperate to tell his mother that such hideous, horrible monsters exist.

Although, as he runs in his now wet and grass-stained Sketchers with the flashing LED lights, he somehow understands that she already knows.

Semper Fidelis

I guess I would have to say the seed of the idea was planted back in college, that morning, the first time I saw her, her caramel skin dancing in the morning sunlight refracted by the dorm room's cheap blinds. I remember looking at her and thinking, "That's not the girl I went to bed with." But her nakedness, the intimate way she was holding me, the lingering combination of her scent and mine blended in a fecund echo of sex left no doubt that she at some point in the night had joined in the festivities.

What was her name? Sabrina? Secara? No. Sedepha? Yeah, I think that was it. Sedepha. I lay there in that bed, trying not to wake her up, not wanting to talk into the uncertainty, just trying to remember the previous night. There were flecks of it, pieces, none of them the ones I wanted. Then, in full-throated recall, I remembered the DJ, over the loudspeaker at O-Malley's: "This last song's for Pete. He's headed out to Saudi tomorrow!"

And it all came back. The failed ice-breakers, the cold shoulders, the smirks and sneers of stuck-up sorority bitches, the frustratingly-long waits at the three-deep bar. And then the imp of an idea. A perverse one, yes, but under the circumstances—and by circumstances, I mean being nineteen, blue-balled, and very drunk—hardly *that* blame-worthy. Why don't we call it an impulsive indiscretion of youth?

I remember tapping the shoulder of the Phi Beta in line in front of me, and yelling into his ear through the miasma of drunken conversation and Billy Joel's *Piano Man,* "Hey man, would you mind if I cut ahead? I'm getting deployed tomorrow. Trying to down a few pitchers with my buds before I have to go to Kuwait."

I don't know if I actually expected it to work. Like I said before, it was just a perversity really.

But work it did, let me tell you. Not only did Greek Boy let me cut him in line, he bought the pitcher. And the shots of Jaeger that accompanied it. In fact, I didn't buy another drink the rest of the night, letting word-of-mouth work its way through the bar. And when that started to lose momentum, I'd just repeat the line: "I'm getting deployed tomorrow." A line more magical, it turns out, than "Open, Sesame."

Now, you might find it hard to believe this worked, but you have to understand that I looked the part. Even more than I do now. I had spent the last few months sublimating the frustrations of the dating scene (or lack of one) into bench presses and arm curls at the gym, so I was pretty cut. And about a month before, I hit the barber for the old Dolph Lundgren flat-top. In short, I *looked* like a Marine.

And you have to remember that, not only are we talking about drunk college students here, but drunk college students at a time of enflamed national fervor. Our President had just told us on CNN that, "This aggression will not stand, this aggression toward Kuwait." So when word got out that I was one of the self-appointed, a bulwark to this aggression, well, let's just say that instead of the off-tune drunken singing of "American Pie"—the normal soundtrack for O'Malley's as last-call approached—there were chants of "Kill Saddam," slaps on the back, encouragement to "get those camel-fuckers," and the *pièce de résistance*, finally getting the DJ to play a request. Somewhere in there, I guess I met Karen, who decided it was her patriotic duty to send me off with a good fuck. And apparently Karen had an Indian roommate named Sedepha. And at some point, apparently, East decided to meet West, with me in the glorious middle.

Do I regret it? Don't know that I do. Sure, there are things that I'm not proud of. Like that my first threesome can only be surmised. Or that when—after an entire sophomore year of trying to break through—I finally get the DJ's attention, I ask for Styx's "Come Sail Away." But I can't say I have any regrets beyond that. The idea, as I think you'll agree, has been quite good to me.

Still, like I said at the start, that morning it was just a seed, accidentally planted. It wasn't anything in the way of an actual, fully-formed curriculum. That came later.

And even that, when it finally came, was every bit as whimsically serendipitous as that night in O'Malley's. When it came, I was in Arlington, Texas. At The Ballpark. Isn't that just the perfect name for a baseball stadium? The Ballpark. Now we have all these stadiums and arenas named after corporations. I remember when they had names that *meant* something? Like War Memorial Stadium. Now it's crap like Charmin Field at Vandalay Industries Arena. I tell ya, kid, nothing's sacred anymore.

This would have been somewhere around 2002 or so. About a year after those *jihad* motherfuckers crashed into the Towers (again with the camel-fuckers! What is it about those people?). So, the P.A. guy asks everyone to stand and remove their hats for the National Anthem, like they always do, when I hear him add, "Active duty and veterans, please salute." They could have been saying that forever for all I knew, but until then, I hadn't heard it. But I sure as shit heard it that day. And I remembered that night in O'Malley's. I figured, "What the hell? Why not? Who'd know?"

And it was just like the bar (without the threesome, unfortunately). Didn't buy a beer or a hot dog that entire game. Was treated with reverence, consideration, and respect. And it felt good. Felt really good.

It didn't take too long to wonder how far I could go with this. I mean, free drinks are nice, but after a while, you want more, you know? But you can't just go around, saluting every flag you see and expect a reward. So, you have to up your game, see? Fortunately, there's Army/Navy stores everywhere, to help you perfect the look. But you also gotta do your research, and that takes some work. Sure, you can get the basic details you need to get started off of Google, names of places served, companies and divisions and whatnot. But for the depth you really need, you gotta go hang out at a local American Legion. The old-timers give the jargon, and from the twitchy PTSDers from the second Gulf War, jumping every time a door slams, you get the real horrorshow stories. How the shit went down in Mosul, a checkpoint ambush at Al Qadisiayh, the Task Force 20 raid that killed Saddam's sons.

It's really not that hard. It's not like you had to memorize their entire story. You just need a few key details, and you let your creativity fill in the rest. Like telling a good joke. And if you trip yourself up, the beauty of it all is that no one presses you. You're one of the valiant, after all. The stricken hero. And if your memory gets a little fuzzy, well, that can only be expected, can't it? War is hell. And if you get *really* stuck, if someone calls you out on a part that doesn't fit, or seems off, you give your story a hard right, talk about the I.E.D., the one that tore your best bud Jimmy in half, whip up some tears, and, believe me, they back off, order you another drink in embarrassment.

Sure, it's not an ideal life. It has its hardships. I decided long ago that it would not be prudent to hang around in one place for too long. A rolling stone gathers no moss, am I right? So, I moved around a lot. Moving from town to town; walking in local parade after local parade.

But it's not like the nomad life doesn't offer its compensations. You get to see the country. Get a rich, deep feel for all it has to offer. The sights, the people, and the collective spirit that makes us so great, so worth fighting for. And of course. there are other, more tangible perks.

Like I said before, I can't remember the last time I paid for a meal. And the women? Let's just say that Karen's sense of patriotic duty is not a rare thing. It's a beautiful thing, no doubt about that, but thankfully, it's not a rare thing.

Of course, where you really clean up isn't at the small-town parades. That's good for a few lunch-specials, a few beers, but mainly just a nice, satisfying inflation of the ego. It's the gun shows that are the thing. Let me tell you, you have never seen the ejaculate of patriotic fervor like you will at a gun show. And if you know what you're doing, you can turn that shit into cold, hard, cash. You can do the "down-on-your-luck veteran" bit, or you can go the spokesman route. Either way, cash in your pocket.

And you still get the ego boost. Everyone tripping over themselves, practically jizzing in their shorts to honor your service. Don't matter the kind of service. You could have machine-gunned a bunch of elderly dinks at My Lai, raped some *burka*-wearing cunt in Tikrit, it don't matter. Hell, I could tell these folks that I skull-fucked some little girl hours before we went into Tora Bora (I like to claim Afghanistan too), and as long as my gun (either one, or both of them, ha!) was wrapped up in the Stars and Stripes, they couldn't give two shits about it.

Now don't look at me that way. I didn't create the system. The grand military-industrial complex. Eisenhower did. What? Well, it don't matter who did it, I'm just saying it wasn't me. I'm just taking advantage of opportunities as I see 'em. That's the American way, ain't it? And don't you start in on the "Truth and Honor" crap, either. I can see in your eyes that's what you're thinking. Let me tell you something: "Truth" and "Honor" are just the fuel that keeps the machine running.

Am I worried about getting caught? Ha. Let me tell you something, kid. If I've learned anything about people through all of this, it's that they want their stories the way they want them. Now, you ordered your eggs sunny-side up; I order mine over-easy. You see what I'm getting at? People want simple. And me? Oh, you bet your grandma's just-fucked ass I'm simple.

And anyway, if someone *does* start to look a little too hard, well, it's a pretty easy thing to persuade them not to. Public sentiment is a cudgel, my friend. Questioning a veteran's story? Challenging his account? After all he's given? After all his sacrifices? How dare you! You see what I'm getting at? It's an easy shame. And if it ever needs that little extra push? You just act out a little PTSD episode and, my friend, you carry the day. So, no, kid, I don't worry about being caught. The fact of *me* says more about them than it does about myself. And that keeps me safe. That keeps me secure. And I prosper. Land of opportunity, right, kid? Land of opportunity.

Why am I telling *you* all of this? That's a fair question. Because it's a good story. One I can't tell as often as I'd like. It's got a real American success edge to it, don't you think? It's kinda like that guy in that Poe story: sometimes you just have to tell someone where the body is, you know what I mean, kid. The perfect crime ain't the perfect crime if no one knows about it.

And besides, you can do fuck-all about it. You try, and there's that cudgel I was talking about. Why, I just have to stand, recite the Pledge of Allegiance, or sing "I'm Proud to Be an American," or some such shit, maybe give my little Purple Heart here (thank God for Ebay, am I right?), a little flick so everyone in here notices it, and, son, that cudgel will soon be beating on your ass. You need to remember, son, you're just a civilian. And me? Well, I'm something else entirely.

Now there are some people, in some circles, who will tell you that this here reflexive patriotism is a problem; some will even say it's dangerous. But I tell you, kid, from where I sit, it's a thing of beauty. Pure fucking beauty. I never get tired of barking out a *"semper fi."* That always gets a rise out of people. I don't know what it is; maybe the arcanity of the language, or just something about individuals living by a code that mystifies them, but believe me, kid, *"semper fi"* is the key. *Semper Fidelis.* Always Faithful.

And the best part is that no one ever thinks to ask, faithful to whom, faithful to what?

<u>Ripples</u>

1

The samurai, battered, broken, bleeding, limps to the edge of the lake. Behind him, the dead and dying litter the battlefield, still shrouded in morning fog. The wound in his side, taut and caked now, pulls at each step. Slowly, he lowers himself onto a fallen tree nestled against a large rock at the water's edge. Crows and larger carrion birds have found the battlefield. Their caws and squawks drown out the moans of the dying. Soon, he knows, the dogs will arrive for their grand share, and comrades and enemies alike, all once vessels of honor, will become nothing but meat. Renownless meat.

Sitting at the water's edge, Tatsuo considers the arrow shaft protruding from his thigh. Because it gives him something to do, postpones the decision that is now his, the samurai unsheathes his *tanto* and cuts the arrow's fletching away, then, since the arrow is buried deep within, he, teeth gritted, pushes the shaft down further into his flesh, grabs the gore-stained head when it emerges, pulls the shaft through his wound.

He contemplates the blood pooling at his feet, the waves of the lake gently lapping at its edges in communion. The pool is large, fulsome. Too large to be accounted for by the arrow's exit wound. Reaching across his body with the right hand, the hand that still has all five fingers, he feels beneath the iron *kozane* where earlier the sword blade found flesh. The wound has pulled open again, and his hand is quickly painted. A veteran of wounds, his body cartographied by scars, he understands this is the one that has killed him.

His mind begins to wander, calling up morning battle scenes and their harmonies, *katanas* crashing against *yoroi*, some sliding off with a metallic scream, others

63

finding purchase on limb, stomach, or head. The gurgle of thrusts, the rip of flesh, the incongruous faint song of a skylark that reached him between combats.

Tatsuo focuses on his diaphragm and breathes. Breathes until his head is clear. He invites the sound of water to absorb him, to lend these last moments a tranquility. Fatigued and weak from blood loss, the samurai slips off the log, landing with his back against the rock. His movement startles a frog; ripples lodge its protest. Pain jars out his calm, allowing one scene of the battle to enter and replay in his mind. The decapitation of his *diamyō*, over and over, each repetition a clarion demanding Tatsuo fulfill his tradition-bound duty. Without his lord, he is now *rōnin*, and there is only one way to remove this shameful stain.

A crane stands at a distant shore-edge, bill poised, waiting, watching, waiting. Soon, the susurrus of frogs resumes. With the two fingers remaining to his left hand, he pries loose a pebble from the wet shore and tosses it into the pellucid before him. Silently, pensively, Tatsuo watches the concentric ripples expand. Idly fondling the green weave of his *tanto* handle, he eyes the crane once more, then returns his gaze to the ripples, bouncing off shorelines, enfolding themselves within each other, collapsing in only to expand again, a shimmered phantasmagoria encompassing all.

2

Sounds.

They drew the young boy to the closed-in porch that ran along the back of the house. Clanking and banging. Muffled talk sprinkled with words he knew were "dirty." Scraping. The susurrus of particulate falling onto plastic.

At first, the young boy was confused, because no one was there. Only a translucent tarp, onto which black ash occasionally fell.

He could make out the voices of his father and grandfather, disembodied but present. Drawn to the voices, the boy approached the tarp. There was a black pipe, a hole in the ceiling, directly above it. Occasionally the boy would glimpse parts of his father through it. His arm, draped in flannel, his jawbone, set and determined in a grimace-grinned sickle, his sweat-matted hairline.

"Daddy, what are you doing?"

It took the boy's father a moment to locate his son's voice, then, looking down through the hole, a Jehovah, he replied.

"Your grandfather and I are trying to replace the chimney for the wood burning stove. Now move away from there, this is dangerous."

"I want to help."

The father smiles at the mild disobedience. "You can't help with this. Just go play."

And the young boy would have. But just as he was about to leave the porch, another ashfall splashed the tarp, and the boy had an idea. A wonderful idea. What fun it would be to be on the bottom of the next fall, to have the ash fall on him like black snow.

So he goes back into the room, lies directly beneath the pipe, and giggles as the ash falls on his face. It tickles.

"Kenny!" his grandmother barks from the kitchen, two rooms away, "you get out from there *this instant*!"

When he sits up, the pipe entire crashes down. He is old enough to understand his head, had it still been there, would have been crushed, and young enough to think that was exciting.

He runs into the kitchen to tell his grandmother that she has saved his life, but there is no one in the kitchen. His grandmother, Kenny's father tells him, is out shopping with his mother. She returns, package-laden, two hours later, and is unable to follow her grandson's hurried, frantic tale of timely warnings and crashing pipes.

Five years later, Kenny, now twelve-years-old, is again in the porch, sitting in front of the glass sliding door that opens onto the stained deck, the in-ground pool, and the woods beyond. His grandmother is also in the room, enjoying the late afternoon sun while she watches her shows. Kenny's father is at work; his mother is in the kitchen prepping dinner. The grandfather is in a well-maintained plot adjoining St. Luke's.

Kenny is sitting in front of the sliding glass door, working a model, a black and white car. His mother told him to move from the kitchen table awhile ago, the fumes of the glue making her mildly queasy.

Kenny is sitting in front of the sliding glass door, using the late afternoon sun to maximize light as he fuses a particularly troublesome connection of chassis and body.

"I better move," Kenny tells the porch, and leaves the model pieces where they lay. It takes him four, maybe five seconds to cross over to the wood-burning stove, a tea-kettle shrieking atop, spitting at the cold, dry, winter air.

Berta, the family's mastiff, barrels through the sliding glass door, sharding the afternoon sun with prism and blood. Although the family will never know this, Berta was wandering the woods back of the pool when some vagrant found a moment of amusement in throwing a lit cherry bomb at the dog. Untethered by fear, Berta bounded back to the house, not registering the glass door, pellucid after a morning's cleaning.

The model car is crushed beneath.

But Berta's story is a happy one. Veterinarians were able to stitch up her many, many cuts, and although she lost much blood, she recovers, and lives out a long, almost-fully happy, dog life.

When the family recounts this harrowing tale of familial minutiae, they express wonder at Kenny knowing at *that* precise moment to get up. How, they marvel, did he know, just then, to move? Ultimately, they conclude he must have seen Berta barreling towards the door, for that is the simplest explanation, and often that is what we seek.

Although he never tells anyone this, Kenny did not see the dog coming. He moved because the voices told him to. The voices that saved him from being crushed by a chimney-pipe five years ago, and that now saved him from being cut to shreds. He has come to rely on the voices. At night, they whisper they will always be there for him.

Two years later, Berta gave birth to her first litter; nine bounding pups. The family decides to keep one of them, the runt. They name him Underdog, after Kenny's favorite cartoon when he was a young, pre-chimney-fallen boy. They will sell or otherwise find homes for the other eight.

But before any of this can happen, Kenny awakes early one morning, puts collar and leash on Berta and leads her through the woods to the back acre, where a muddy stream cuts through the property. He ties her to an oak, pats her on the head, gives her a treat.

"Good girl," he praises her. "Stay. I'll be right back. Stay."

And he does come back, three times. The first two, he carries large cardboard boxes that welp and wriggle. On the third trip, he brings nine burlap sacks. Into each sack, he places one of the pups, along with a stone gathered from the stream bed. He ties the sack with butcher's twine taken from the kitchen.

"Hey, Berta. Say good-bye to Underdog," he says, before tossing the first sack into the stream, swollen and whooshing from days of rain previous.

He does this eight times more, naming each pup in turn, a christening and a requiem simultaneous.

He understands he should feel bad about what he's done. But the voices are there, encouraging, whispering, reminding him that this was the only way to make Berta, the ungrateful bitch, pay.

3

Meiko was at the stream washing clothes when a winded young boy brought news of the arrival of the *diamyō* with his fighting men. She, along with the other women and the children playing nearby, rushed back to the village to see. The soldiers marching through the village on foot, laden with arrows and with bows astride, were just men; but the samurai on horseback, they seemed to Meiko something else. Half monster man-gods, the horns of their *kabutos* piercing the sky, sun glinting off the scales of armor; they were dragon men, and Meiko trembled involuntarily in awe and fear.

One among them drew her attention. His *kozane* scales alternating red and black, a single sickle-bladed moon across his helmet, he called all eyes to him the way a mountain does. Meiko found herself weaving among the crowd, keeping pace with the samurai's horse. Then she saw his eyes. Meiko gasped, for there could be no mistake. One eye green as emerald, the other a deep brown. This was Tatsuo, the one they whisperingly called *"Futari No Tamashi,"* "Two Souls." Some said the green eye was that of a demon who gifted Tatsuo with great strength and skill in battle; others that the brown eye, the color of a scabbed-over wound, contained the soul of Tatsuo's first battle-enemy, who offered his vanquisher a spare life. To kill Tatsuo, they whispered, you must kill him twice. He was the most honored, most loved, and most feared among the *diamyō*'s men. He strode upon his bay mare behind his lord, out into the field adjacent the village where the soldiers were to camp.

Meiko watched him dismount and hand the reins to his page. By chance, their gazes overlap, and Meiko felt something reach across the field, pierce into her stomach, grab her insides, twist and release them, over and again. Twist, hold, release, a knot unloosed and retied, a caterpillar re-cocooned. Over and again. Against this collapse, she smiled. And Tatsuo, "Dragon Man," "Two Souls," this great warrior, this killer of hundreds of men, smiled back.

When Meiko joins her father and mother for the midday meal, her stomach still flutters, both empty and full. As they eat, her father mentions that, while the soldiers will camp in the field, it is expected that the villagers will billet the samurai. Meiko thinks of Tatsuo sleeping in this house, her house, and blushes. She hopes her father does not see.

Near the end of the meal, Meiko cannot help herself. She turns to her father. Crafting her words with things that mattered to men, she says, "it would be a great honor if Tatsuo were billeted with us."

"Tatsuo?" her mother interrupts. "The one they call 'Two Souls? No, I do not wish for that. I would not be able to sleep with that man in this house. They say he is a demon.'"

Meiko knows that she too would not be able to sleep with that man in the house. Again, she blushes and again hopes her father does not see.

"He is not a demon," she says.

"Httt," the father grunts an intrusion. He insinuates with a glance at the cane propped against the wall that this is an inappropriate conversation for women to have. But perhaps because the arrival of the army has brought with it a celebratory atmosphere, or perhaps because the thoughts and desires of women elude him, he decides to be benevolent. Neither woman will feel the cane today, he decides.

Meiko sits on a bench outside her home. She is painting watercolors when a shadow darkens the canvas. Looking up, Meiko sees Tatsuo standing above her.

"There are no cranes like that where I am from," he says, pointing at her orange and pink bird. "Where I am from, the cranes are all white."

"There are no cranes like this here, either," Meiko replies.

Something about the response pleases Tatsuo and he smiles. "What is your name?" he asks.

"Meiko."

"You should be painting a flower, then."

"A crane is a moving flower."

Tatsuo considers this.

"And there *could* be cranes like this, somewhere," Meiko decides into the silence. "One day I shall go look for them."

Tatsuo smiles at the fantasy. "You will let me know if you find one."

"If the *diamyō* is slain in the battle to come," Meiko said, blushing at her boldness, "you could look for them yourself. You would be *rōnin*. You could wander."

Tatsuo's smile recoils. "How can you say such things? The *diamyō* slain! And to be *rōnin* carries great shame."

"To be *rōnin* is freedom."

"It is to be without honor. To wander, my child, is to be lost."

"There are *rōnin* who have kept their honor."

Tatsuo smiles indulgently. "You are thinking, no doubt, of The Forty-Seven. How old are you, Mieko?"

"Fourteen."

"Then you are old enough to know better. The Forty-Seven is a myth. Nothing more. Just a story to entertain children."

"Maybe so. But it is a good story."

"I think you forget how that story ends, little Meiko."

"It didn't need to end that way. It could have ended differently and still be true. Beautiful and true."

"Like your crane?"

"Yes. Like my crane."

Tatsuo looks up at the house. "Your father watches us."

"He will use the cane tonight."

"You do not sound afraid."

"He thinks my tears make him strong. He does not understand that tears are just forgotten rain. But tonight, I will not cry. I will stay in the place he cannot touch."

Tatsuo stands before the girl, silent, considering. He reaches out a hand, and into it Meiko decides to place the painting. Tatsuo turns to leave, stops. "Not all men seek strength that way," he says.

"That is also a good story."

"Like your crane?"

"Yes, like my crane."

4

Jessica had strong opinions about the existence of monsters, having given birth to one. For a long time, she refused to see that's what he was. But denial became harder after what he did to the McMurtry girl. And then, when the school principal called all the parents on the way home from that tragic field trip into the city, letting them know that counselors would be made available to any student traumatized by what happened to that woman on the subway platform, Jessica somehow knew. It was not an accident. That woman didn't commit suicide, didn't jump in front of that train. She was pushed. And in the pit of her stomach, she knew her son did the pushing. And on the heels of that realization came a second, this one more soul-emptying: she was terrified, afraid of her own son.

Lou wouldn't listen. He never did. "We don't know," he said, years ago, "that Kenny did anything worse than leave a door open and the puppies ran away. We don't know he did anything to them."

"But all of them?" Jessica had countered. "While still nursing?"

And about the McMurtry girl, Lou was even more dismissive. "I saw lots of fights growing up where one kid bit the other."

"But so many bites. The other kids said it was like he was trying to actually eat her."

"He just got carried away, is all."

But she knew none of this was normal. No mother should be afraid of her own child. It took Kenny punching her in the stomach, hard, the day she and Lou told him he'd be having a baby brother in seven months, for Lou to admit something was wrong. It took the fear of a miscarriage to open his eyes and agree with Jessica that it was time to explore options. Aggressive options. And then progressively more aggressive options.

For the past two years, she lived with the guilt of committing her own flesh to a mental hospital. A guilt only slightly less haunting than knowing, if her suspicions about the subway platform were true, that she may have waited too long to do it, her negligence perhaps costing a life.

Then she got the letter. Just one handwritten line: "Be home soon! Can't wait to see you, Momma!"

After calming her with Sauvignon Blanc and Xanax, Lou called the state hospital and confirmed that Kenny, twenty-years old now and, according to his dismissal chart, symptom-free for more than a year, had been free for almost a week.

"Why, then, hasn't he come here?" Jessica asked.

"Because he doesn't plan to, Jess. You have nothing to worry about."

She hated when he called her "Jess" and hated the smooth way he latched onto an explanation and immediately made it gospel. Always in control and always right. In the months that followed the letter, Lou didn't think twice about it and Jessica thought of nothing else. Every day when she returned from work, she could barely summon the courage to walk inside, convinced that Kenny was lurking in some corner, hiding in some closet. Sometimes, she just waited in the car until Lou came home, pretending she got stuck in traffic and pulled in just moments before he did.

Tonight, when the wine and Xanax weren't enough to settle the fear of being in the house alone, Lou told her over the phone to take a nice, relaxing bath. "I'll be home in a few hours. Tops. I promise."

After checking and re-checking the locks on the doors and windows and refilling her wine glass, Jessica eased herself into the near-scalding water and tried to calm herself. "You have nothing to worry about," Lou said to her when the letter came; she let that promise echo through her head as she watched water droplets fall off her raised foot. The tiny impacts sent ripples billowing across the steaming water, ambiguous undulations encapsulating everything and nothing.

The water and the candles began their magic. Jessica closed her eyes, sank deeper into the tub and remembered peace. Through the thin shades of her eyelids, she became aware of light, wavering, dancing. For several moments, her relaxed mind assumes candleflame, then, gradually, she processes its intensity, its direction, and she knows.

Sitting upright, bathwaves rolling out onto the floor in repeating rushes, Jessica saw an unsteady brightness break the rectangle night of the bathroom window. Rushing to her feet, not bothering with robe or towel, she looked out, and there he was, waving up at her.

"Hi, Momma!"

The windows of the front floor vomit flame and smoke. Jessica wraps her hand in a washcloth and tries the door handle. She can barely budge the door.

From the front yard, Kenny continues, "They remembered where Daddy hides the key."

She slams her shoulder against the door again and again. In the crack her useless collisions she creates, she sees the dressers jammed against the door.

"This house tried to kill me! Tried to crush my head with a chimney, Momma. And what about you? You put me away. You shouldn't have done that. That's not what Mommas do."

Kenny's eyes glaze over as he watches the flames ascend. From her pyre, Jessica sees him cock his head as if listening intently to something. A beat later, he nods. Jessica sees him smile, and then clap his hands with childlike joy.

"They say it's my birthday now, Momma! Yay! Happy birthday to me! Blow out the candles, Momma. Hahahaha. Blow out my candles, Momma, and make a wish."

5

When the drunk-driver T-boned her car four years ago, Lily should have died. Would have too, if not for seven units of donated blood. And because of that donation, every ninety days since her recovery, she makes an appointment at the Keystone Blood Center to pay back this anonymous debt.

These are solemn events for her. The appointments counted out in January, written into her daily planner in ink. She allows herself no surge of gratification, no smug self-promoting stickers on shirt or jacket, no pride over the doing of good deeds. It wasn't about her. It was the recognition of an obligation, the balancing of a ledger.

"Right as rain."

The voice intruded into her silence as she lay in the recovery room. On the bed next to her was an old man. Ghost-white hair surrounding tonsure-like baldness, a lush Fu Manchu, blue-and-white flannel shirt flared around a weathered white T-shirt, faded jeans that looked just slightly younger than he was. Eyes so green they seemed concave. Lily recognized him from previous visits, always talking the ear off another donor or one of the nurses.

"Excuse me?" she said.

"I said, 'right as rain.' That's you. Every ninety days, right as rain."

"Well, this is important to me. Because . . ." she faltered, unsure if she felt like sharing.

"No matter the 'because.' Don't much matter the *whys* of doing good, s'long as you got the *whens* and the *hows* of doing it. Name's Chester Earl," he added after a pause. He took a sip of the soda the nurses forced on them, took a bite of cookie, and considered Lily as he chewed. "Did I ever tell you 'bout the gator?"

"Excuse me?" Lily said again.

"The gator I pulled out of the Jordan Creek here about, well, let me see, must have been two decades back near about."

"No. You never told me about the gator."

"Well," Chester said, a slight twinkle in his eye, "ain't that something."

He smiled and he began:

"Back then, I was working animal control. Job like any other, I suppose. Paid regular, had its share of ups and downs. Didn't much like the thought of those cats and dogs getting put down, "euthemized" they called it, but you also got to reunite pets with their owners from spell to spell, and that was always something. And even those euthemized ones, well, sometimes you could get them nice and calmed, pettin' 'em, talking softly to 'em. Tellin' 'em everything would be OK. Give 'em a sense of peace, knowin' what they's headed for. That was always something, too, I suppose.

But the story I aim to tell you ain't about dogs or cats or anything regular like that. Someone called in a report of seeing a gator lurking in the Jordan Creek, out back near the Wildlife Preserve they got there. Well, of course, no one really believed that report, but still, we had to check it out just the same. And sure 'nough, there she was, just at the shore edge near where they had Jim Parsons put in that stone footbridge back in '75 or '6, can't quite remember which.

And I don't mean any little pet store gator. This was a full-grown lady. Six feet if she was an inch. Maybe six and a half, not quite seven. And let me tell you, she was a sight to see. A Gator. In Pennsylvania. Just floating there like the most natural thing in Creation. If you didn't believe in miracles, well, this here would give you something to chew on.

For a spell, I just sat and watched her. She was beautiful, I tell you. Thought long and hard about leaving her be. But then, families picnic down there, kids go fishing, and there was the concern about the colder months coming. A Pennsylvania winter could sure cause her a world of problems, the way I figured it.

If they sent someone else, I suppose they'd've just gone and shot her and gone about their day, but I never gave that no thought. I also suppose I should've could've called for help, but back then I was getting to that age when you still care 'bout what people think, want to show 'em you still got it, can still do it without no help.

We kept one of them poles with them wire-nooses on the end, for catching snakes and such, so I figure if I could get close enough I could slip that over her snout, cinch it shut; then it would just be a matter of wrestling her into the truck back.

And more or less, that's how it happened. Whadn't easy, I'll tell you that. Near 'bouts two-hundred and fifty pounds of pissed off—excuse me—reptilian. I don't think I've ever lifted and carried half that weight before, but somehow, not really sure how, I got her into the truck back.

But let me tell you, fishing a gator out of a creek is one thing. It's another all together what to do with it once you got it. And that's the problem I had.

First, I called that zoo they have there up on the other side of the preserve. I half thought the gator must have been theirs anyway, and if it wasn't, figured they'd want one. Wrong on both 'counts. Spent the rest of the day calling 'bout any place I could think of. Called that aquarium down cross the river from Philly, handful of zoos, couldn't get a straight answer out of any of them, lessen that answer was "no."

By this time, everyone and anyone round 'bout the place was telling me to just put her down, but they's never saw her in that creek bed. So tranquil. Majestic, I'd call it. Full of awe kinda stuff, you know? Didn't seem right to put her down. The way I figured, wasn't only one thing to do with her. Decided then and there I'd drive her down to

Florida, find a nice secluded gator-friendly stretch of swamp or creek, and let her go.

And that's what I did. Duct-taped her snout shut, had one of them reptile expert fellas on the phone—forget what they're called, there's some fancy-type name for 'em—he tells me to keep her wet. Also told me to put some tape over her eyes, that that'd calm her down. Don't know how they know that, but it did seem to work regular like.

Left that night. Figured it'd take me somewheres 'round seventeen, eighteen hours, way my truck runs. One of the things that sticks with me still is that I had one damn cassette tape with me. Manfred Mann. I listened to "Blinded by the Light" and "The Mighty Quinn" over and again until I knew I'd be just fine never hearing them again. All just to bring that damn—excuse me again—gator back where I thought it belonged.

Now the gator ain't really the story, or leastwise, it ain't the only part. Round 'bout 2 or 3 in the a.m., I'm in North Carolina, forty miles or so south of Fayetteville, when I see a man and a boy on the highway, hitchhiking. Boy couldn't have been more'n eight or nine. I stop and let 'em in, tell 'em I'm headed south to Florida. They don't seem to have much care where I'm going; seem more interested in moving than in any 'ticular direction.

I remember they smelled of wood smoke, the both of them. Like they was sitting 'fore a big fire for a spell. I didn't ask them nothing 'bout it, not wanting to pry into matters that ain't mine, so we just talk a bit about this and a bit about that and a bit about nothing in particular. Just small talk, mind you. We're coming up on the Georgia border, and the man sets to crying. Not the blubbering of great grief, but constrained sobbing, like he's losing a debate he needed to win. Generally speaking, I don't like to intrude much into other's people's affairs, like I said, but when there's a stranger crying in your truck in the middle of a night, you kinda have to notice.

'You all right, brother,' I says to him, and he nods like and tries to pull himself together. But after a few miles, he set to it again. So, I ask him again, and he tells me he's sorry.

'Ain't no need to 'pologize for crying. Ain't no shame in it,' I says.

He then tells me it ain't the crying he's sorry for, but the robbing. Takes out a hunting knife from a pocket in his jacket, tells me to pull over to the shoulder, and give him my wallet. Boy's crying in the backseat the whole time, 'Daddy, don't do this. Daddy, don't do this.'

He looks back at the boy and says, 'I got to. We ain't got no choice. We ain't got nothing anymore.'

Looking back at his boy must have been what got him thinking about the truck back, 'cause he then asks me what I got back there. I tell him, and he says he'll be needing that too. Don't know why he wanted her; don't know what he thought he'd do with her. Suppose he thought he'd kill her and sell the pelt somewheres, get a few extra bucks that way.

Now I weren't without some protection. I had me in my truck, or at least I used to in 'dem days, this ol' knife like thing. Called them "Tontos" or some such. Like the Lone Ranger's pal. My daddy brought it home with him from Guadalcanal back in the war. So it was sitting there, right next me, green handle poking up from between the seat and belt. But I never gave no thought to it. Always figured it as more ornamentation-like than anything else.

Instead, I told him, 'You can put that knife away. You don't need it. Now, I'll give you my money, gladly. You be needing it a whole lot more'n I do, sounds like. And there's a sack of groceries and the like back there next to your boy. Sandwiches and such. You go ahead and take that, too. But what I got in the truck back? That I can't give you. Ain't mine to give. And you're gonna just have to accept that, or decide to up the ante higher 'n you planned. I'm hopin' you'll do the former.'

He didn't say nothing to that right away. Just sat there quietly. Did put the knife away, though, which I took as a good sign. Then he mumbled something. Didn't quite catch what it was, and was 'bout to ask him to repeat it. But then I figured he done had enough shame for a night. I reached into the back seat for the sack of food. He took it and was 'bout to open the door.

'Ain't no need to hop out here. I can take you to the next gas station. Let you out there.'

And that's how it happened, the both of them crying quietly until we reached a Shell station and off they went. To what end, I never knew. I think 'bout that, 'bout them, from time to time. I suppose they made out all right.

The immediate problem I had, though, was that without any money for gas, I couldn't make it to Florida. Wound up stopping somewheres above the Okefeenokee right before dawn. I don't suppose she minded, though. Not sure there's much difference between Florida swamp and Georgia swamp. And seeing her bolt into that water? Well, I can't say with a certainty she was happy, 'cause I don't know if that's part of reptilian nature, but she seemed, well, 'bout the only word I can come up with is 'proper.' As she burst into that water, like a firecracker the moment it goes off, that gator seemed proper.

And even though she nipped two fingers as I cut the tape from around her snout, even though I had to work odd jobs here and there for the next week to get enough for gas home, I felt warm and full watching her go off. I sat down on a tree stump and watched her disappear. Watched the ripples of her wake bounce around, ricochet against each other, and then slowly subside. And I'll be damned if I didn't feel proper too."

***

His tale told, Chester Earl returned to the soda and the cookie.

"That's a sad story," Lily said finally.

"Well, that there's the thing. I'm not sure it is. And I'm not sure it's not. I had an older brother. Earl Chester, if you can believe that. Our folks weren't none too creative when it came to namin'. And he was the meanest son of a bitch to walk the earth. The kind that would take two alley cats, tie their tails together and toss them over a clothesline, the kind that would throw firecrackers at dogs, sleep with other men's wives. Growing up, I used to think I had to undo his meanness by being good. That it was all on me. Now, I'm not sure it mattered, one way or the other."

Chester Earl stood, polished off his soda, popped the rest of the cookie into his mouth, and chewed it with an amused smile, staring at Lily all the while. He winked, touched his hand to the bill of an imaginary cap. "Obligation's a hell of thing. It can collapse you in, or expand you out, and you can never be sure which is right. All you can be sure of, is that it'll hold you down if'n ain't truly yours" he said, then walked out of the recovery room.

6

After dropping his last rider at the blood bank, Daniel pulled into the Wegman's parking lot. He wants nothing more than to head home, open a bottle of wine, and drink himself to numbness. Or drive over to the Wildlife Preserve, stick his feet in the creek and catch the sunset. But he can't. He's only made $93 today, and needs at least $120 a day to catch up to the monthly bills. So when a ping finally comes in, from Tariq in Breinigsville, Daniel feels obliged to accept it, and begins the plodding drive through truck-thick Rt. 100 towards the industrial complex.

The first thing Daniel finds odd is that Tariq is white. Early twenties, wearing a hoodie and carrying a tattered backpack. Daniel, who is vociferously liberal, chides himself for this reflexive racial assumption.

"Hey, Tariq. Happy to meet you. How are you today?"

Daniel fills the silent void with practical words: "OK, I have the address as 4547 Wildflower Lane, is that right?"

And tries the silence once more: "OK. Great. GPS says it should take us about 13-14 minutes, so you just relax, and enjoy the ride."

This last is merely rehearsed friendliness, honed over months of learning what behaviors are most likely to result in tips. It is not meant to be taken literally, so Daniel is a bit surprised when Tariq stretches his body across the backseat, lifting his head intermittently, just to window level, as if peeking out to see if his departure has been noticed.

While Daniel finds this odd, it is well below the threshold of truly odd things he's seen as an Uber driver, so he drives on. And the rudeness of Tariq's silence, while annoying, is hardly unique. Even when Tariq begins a muttered conversation with himself, with different pitches signifying Question and Answer, Daniel merely raises an eyebrow and drives on.

He has almost completely fallen into that visual white-noise zone that is one of the few perks of this job, a total erasure of attention, just autonomic driving, when Tariq finally speaks: "I need you to pull over."

Daniel eases the car over to the shoulder. A request that is, again, odd but not unique.

"No, not here! They'll see me! Pull over at the next side street."

Daniel wants to ask who "they" are, but intuits the answer will not answer anything, so he silently drives on, pulling onto the next side street and once again easing the car towards the shoulder.

"No! You're not in far enough. They could still see. Drive down farther." Then, because Tariq senses clarification will get him what he wants, he adds, "I'm going to throw up."

Daniel understands and is grateful. While he would get a $200 fee if Tariq pukes in his car, he would still need to clean it up, so he appreciates his rider's desire to avoid this. Daniel drives on and when he is deep down the street, with no possibility of anyone on the main road seeing, he eases the car to the shoulder for the third time.

Tariq cries as he vomits, and in between sobs and retches, resumes his mumbled conversation. Daniel has now grown weary of the weirdness, and just wants to get the ride over with. The GPS indicates 4547 Wildflower Lane is a mere three minutes away.

He pulls back onto the main street, crests a hill, and casually notes that at the hill's bottom, a State Trooper has a car pulled over.

"Oh, fuck! Fuck, fuck, fuck, fuck!" Tariq yells from the back seat. He then frantically unzips his backpack and plunges his hand inside.

Before Daniel can ask obvious questions, there is a peripheral flash, late afternoon sun glinting off the snubbed barrel of the pistol now on Tariq's hand.

Time slows down for Daniel. He registers that it's a .38 revolver; that all six cylinders are filled; that Tariq has started to cry again, that his pupils are both bloodshot and dilated, which Daniel never knew was possible; that in between sobs, Tariq is once again muttering to his Confessor. Daniel also understands that, in all probability, he will die within the next few moments. Oddly, this does not upset him. Daniel greets this information as he would the discovery of a new color. He is preternaturally calm.

"Easy, brother," he soothes. "He's not here for you. He's just pulled over a speeder, is all. You just stay chill and I'll have you home in two minutes."

"You can't take me home now. The cops will be there too. Waiting for me."

"There won't be cops waiting. It'll just be your home. Nothing else. You just sit tight and hold on." Then, choosing his words very carefully to cut off needless denial, Daniel adds, "What did you take?"

The needless denial came nonetheless "Nothing. I didn't take nothing."

"I've had some bad trips myself," Daniel lies, "so you just sit tight, brother. I'll get you home. We'll get you through this. Everything will be OK. Proper."

"You can't take me home." Tariq repeats more forcefully.

"OK. OK. I'll take you wherever you want to go. You just tell me where."

"Just drive. Please. Just drive."

"You got it, brother. You just relax, and I'll just drive."

For the next half an hour, Daniel drives along the narrow roads cut into the side of Bear Creek Mountain, some of his favorite roads, roads where you can go long stretches without seeing another car, where you are just a forgotten raindrop sliding along an emerald. Long have these roads given Daniel peace and comfort, and they do so again. He forgets about the revolver still held, distractedly, near his head. He forgets about his drug-addled passenger, and about the fact he could be a nanosecond's misunderstanding from death. He just drives.

After a particularly glorious S-curve through the verdant, Daniel turns to Tariq- "I always love driving on this mountain. Some days you can drive up and down and hardly ever see another car. It's one of my favorite places, to tell you the truth. Do you have a place like that? A place that just calls you to it? Pulls you into position? Where something locks into place and it doesn't matter if you were anxious or weary, you get to this place, and without even knowing it, you sigh, and then, in the blink of an eye, Tranquility finds you."

Tariq does not answer. In the rearview mirror, Daniel stares into Tariq's deep brown eyes. They give nothing back. Tariq tilts his head, as if intently listening to something. A beat later, he nods.

"You can take me home now."

"You sure, brother? You ok now?"

"Yeah. I'm ok now."

Daniel turns around in the next driveway and heads back towards Alburtis. Wildflower Lane is a dirt road winding up another section of the mountain. Becoming increasingly isolated, branches of oak and willow closing over the ever-narrowing road, really little more than two tire ruts by this point. Despite his earlier calmness, Daniel starts to get jittery.

"Um, is the house much farther up?" he asks, hoping his voice stayed firm, did not whisper his unease.

"It's just around the bend, brother."

And maybe it was the tone of Tariq's voice, or his adoption of Daniel's own fraternal phrasing, or the glimpse he caught of the stone-faced house-front, or just the catharsis that follows any emotionally-charged moment, but Daniel felt a profound release. A peace, full and warm. He thinks, now that this is over, he has one hell of a good story to tell. His sigh is long and full. He catches a glimpse of himself in the mirror, smiling.

"Yes," Tariq said softly. "Yes. That's right. Everything's OK. I'm happy for you, Daniel. I'm *so* happy for you."

And then Kenny shot Daniel in the head.

7

When word reached the village that the battle was over, that the *diamyō* and his samurai were all dead, Meiko ran from the house before her father could forbid such a thing. Snarling dogs held the field when she arrived. Only the most desperate pillagers and the most compassionate healers braved the rent and blooded ground. Meiko carefully made her way across the field, afraid to find Tatsuo, afraid not to.

When she had searched the slain and soon-to-be without finding him, a flicker of hope caught purchase and grew within her despite her earlier fear. Maybe Tatsuo had reconsidered, maybe he *was* now wandering, a *rōnin*, free to ever seek, beholden only to himself. The thought filled her with joy, her smile incongruous in the midst of such death surrounding.

But then she saw the trail of blood leading down a footpath away from the field, towards the lake, and somehow, she knew that this trail ended at Tatsuo.

At the lake's edge, she found the samurai's *tantō* in its sheath. Tatsuo's face was soft, still; the body at peace, liquescent. Meiko stared into the samurai's bi-colored eyes, no longer pellucid, and processed his final moments, was glad that he did not have to weigh the value of wandering against the worth of honor. The strength to choose rightly, she realized now, lay beyond him, and she was glad he did not live long enough to learn this. For an interminable while, she sat beside the renowned "Two Souls," emptied now of both.

She does not cry. Instead, she reaches for the *tanto* handle hesitantly, as if afraid it will burn her, then chides herself for this momentary weakness. She reaches once more, pulling the *tanto* free, hefting its weight. Looking across the lake, she sees a crane—the hue of feather trivial—at a distant shore-edge, bill poised, waiting, watching, and she understands. She re-sheaths the *tanto*, unbuckles the samurai's belt, drapes it over her shoulder, and runs. Away from the battlefield, away from the village.

Tatsuo is now irrevocably beholden to place, but Meiko is not. Like a firecracker the moment it goes off, she runs.

8

She waits, patiently, near the shoreline of a boggy creek in backwater Georgia, motionless, submerged. Dragonflies hover above her protruding green-brown eyes, eyes that remain open for an interminable while before a single blink sends faint, virtually-indiscernible ripples across the flat, liquid surface.

She has grown behemoth. And she waits.

For all of the years and all of the reasons and none of the whys, she waits.

Patiently. Peacefully. Properly. For what she knows will come.

She is eternal.

She is inevitable.

She is insatiable.

And she waits.

<u>Once Upon a Time in New Haven</u>

"You ever notice no one gets diarrhea on the Hallmark Channel?" Boner said into the awkward silence of the bus.

"Jesus Christ, Boner," Jaxon replied, "What the actual fuck are you talking about?"

"I'm just saying, you never see it. I mean, my dad gets the shits three, four times a week. You'd think if they wanted a bit of real life on those sappy love shows, every once in a while, someone'd get the squirts."

"Maybe your dad gets the shits four times a week because your mom can't cook."

"Naw, he just eats a lot of Thai food. Says he actually enjoys the next day shit. Calls it 'Hot Ass.'"

"Gil, a little help here," Jaxon said, turning to his other friend. "I can't talk to Boner alone. Gives me a headache. Dilute this nonsense for me, will ya?"

Gil had only been three-quarters listening, intent on the crumpled figure draped across the seats opposite them, fetaled under an army jacket and a dirty blanket, trying to message out the figure's story.

"Gil? Gil, Gil, Gil, Gil, Gil." Each repetition of his name paired with a friendly—but just a bit harder than it needed to be, as was Jaxon's way—punch on the arm.

"Knock it off," Gil said, turning his shoulder and arm away. He gave Jaxon a look that said, 'Who told you to invite Boner anyway?'

"Boner," he said, "what the hell made you think of that?"

"I don't know. I was thinking about jelly, and it kinda just went from there."

Gil shot Jaxon another look, one that said 'See?'

But he also understood Boner. Understood that the comment had nothing to do with jelly. Had nothing to do with the Hallmark Channel or Thai food either. It had everything to do with the fact that Boner had never been on a public bus before, never went to downtown New Haven on his own, without a parent or two (for Boner was lucky enough to still have both). He was nervous. And when Boner was nervous, his penchant for saying things most people found stupid or random or both became unfettered, set loose upon the world without bounds.

"Mary's period-stained panties!" Jaxon swore, "I don't know why we brought you along."

"You're the one who invited me," Boner replied.

"Yeah. But only because you've been staked out in my lawn since they announced school would be closed today, desperately afraid we'd do something without you."

"Well, wouldn't you?"

"You bet your aunt's tight-ass we would've. Bad enough we've got to deal with this wino and his piss-stink," Jaxon gestured at the sleeping form that had held Gil's attention, "but on top of that, we got to listen to you carry on about your father's shits, which, for some fucked-up reason, reminds you of jelly. Remind me never to eat toast at your house."

Jaxon also had never been on a public bus or to downtown New Haven alone. He was also nervous. And when he was nervous, he became aggressive. The Mouse That Roared.

Gil had never been on a public bus before, either. He had been to New Haven a handful of times with his older brother, Stanford, for a slice, sometimes a whole pie. But never anything like this. Never anything this exposed. He was nervous as well, but in a different way than Jaxon or Boner. His was the fluttery euphoria of an adventure well-begun *because* it was begun.

An adventure the seed of which was planted the day before, after the bomb-threat at school. When the announcement came that the authorities had not yet cleared the building, that school would have to be kept closed another day, that they all had a free late-spring day to fill however they liked. The seed, in the form of an off-hand comment from Stanford.

"You guys should go downtown. Go to Cutler's."

Cutler's. The Holy Grail of record stores. A mere whiff of legend to the junior high students in North Haven, dependent as they were on parental transportation. And parents in North Haven, as a whole, did not drive into New Haven, the entire polyglotinous city oversimplified as "the ghetto," the stench of its name, and the knee-jerk socio-economic generalizations an affront to their collective suburban noses. If their sons and daughters want to get music, they could ride their bikes down to Hamden, buy their music at any of the hermetic shopping malls there.

But not today. Today, Gil, Jaxon, and Boner had ridden their bikes to the bus station instead. Paid their fares. And now were riding the bus down State St, pointed directly at the heart of New Haven, at the center of which lay Cutler's, their El Dorado.

"Shut up, man. He'll hear you," Boner whispered at Jaxon's wino comment. "Plus, I don't think he's a wino. I think he's a vet. Check out the jacket."

"I don't give your father's runny shits if he does. And anyone can get an army jacket. It's called an Army/Navy store, dumb-ass."

"No, he earned his," Gil said, pointing at the man's biceps, exposed by a roll-over. The tattoo read, "82nd Airborne. Death From Above."

The roll-over morphed into a wake-up as the man unfurled into a sitting position, blinking his eyes awake. He looked around the bus with burgeoning panic, as if unsure where he was or how he got there. His eyes settled on the boys opposite. The layers of dirt and sweat-grime staining his skin was just slightly fainter than the same stains on his jacket. He seemed to exist in a self-contained atmosphere of cigarette fog and whisky-cloud.

"Hey," he said. "Little dudes. I'm gonna tell you a secret. You wanna know the best way to fuck a chicken? When you're ready to cum, you snap its neck. The death throes, man. The death throes. Push you over the edge every time. Like nothing else."

He then lay back down, rolling himself over like a strip of bacon frying itself. Muttering "the death throes, the death throes" over and again.

The boys exchanged a loaded glance and as one, stood and pulled the cord, deciding they'd walk the rest of the way.

As they stepped down, the man, half-reclaimed by the fog of his terrible memories, muttered into the void where there were once three boys, "it takes a village," he now said over and again. "It takes a village."

With the inversion of logic typical of teenage boys, they decided to have dessert before lunch, turning down Chapel St. then Chestnut, before hanging a right onto Wooster, and they were there. Libby's.

"The best Italian pastry in New England," Stanford told him. "Be sure you stop there," he added, "We always did."

"Hey guys," Boner wheezed behind them, "wait up."

Jaxon contemplated the jiggling effort to catch up, declared, "God damn, you are a fat fuck."

Gil placed his hand on Jaxon's arm, shook his head. "Don't."

"Why not?"

"Just don't. Low hanging fruit."

"About the only fruit that beached whale eats," Jaxon mumbled against the reproof.

"You said it was only four blocks," Boner whined when he reached them.

"And it was," Gil said. "I never said four blocks in a row," he added, winking mollification at Jaxon, today's adventure too grand to blemish with bruised feelings.

For a moment, they just stood outside the glass front, starlights of reflected fluorescence from the illuminated sign dazzling even in the late-morning sun. Inside, Gil knew, would be wonders beyond wonders, a display case cookie kaleidoscope: raspberry finger cookies, milanos, snowballs, tri-color butter, macaroons, thumbprints, cherry-butter, and jewel. Over the years, Gil had tried them all, the whole assortment of traditional Italian cookies. The pastel pinks and greens of star cookies, green acorns smudged with dipped chocolate, the pignolis—that looked like gnarly pieces of shit, but still somehow managed to seduce through the whiff of almond and the promise of pine nut. But he had only had them from boxes of white cardboard, brought home by his mother when elevated company—a boss or her parents—were visiting.

But here was the fount itself. Not the white boxes but where they were folded and filled. The source, the magical source of something he had only been allowed to nibble on. Just a glass doorway away.

"But I don't know anything about Italian pastry," Boner's complaint shattered Gil's reverie.

"It looks to me like you know a whole lot about pastry," Jaxon replied, giving Boner an exaggerated once-over. "I think you'll figure it out, instinctual-like."

Boner looked at his friend with eyes that recorded the sting, then dismissed it.

"I'm sorry about your mother," he said. "I hope she comes back."

The inside of Libby's was even more magical than they imagined. A confectionate fairy-tale land. The cookies, of course, were rainbow-arrayed in their display case, but there was more. Cakes of all kinds filled another display case. Pies too. And the *cannoli*, arrayed and displayed in a case of their own. All the wonders of the world, it seemed, were offered to them; whatever form their particular pleasure took this day was theirs for the asking.

"Let me explain something to you, my little *figa* friend," the man in line before them scolded the worker behind the counter. He was large, dressed in what seemed to Gil like an expensive suit. There was a large, obvious bulge under the suit jacket, where one supposed the heart lay. Resting on top of the bulge, a medallion of St. Christopher, dangling from the gold chain around the man's neck. His pomaded hair the black of the universe. He was holding a small white paper bag, into which he looked from time to time, as if mystified by its contents, as if one final glance would disprove the evidence of his eyes. There was around him an atmosphere that Gil couldn't touch, but knew he didn't want to. A collective of the assembled hurts of the world, drizzled in a nectar of savage significance.

"I ordered three *cannoli* and a lobster tail. I even pointed at them in the case. Now, you gave me the lobster tail. Congratulations. And you put three *cannoli* into the bag. Again, my congratulations. But tell me if you see any difference here." He pulled two of the *cannoli* from the bag, one brimmed with ricotta and cream filling, the other one laden with mocha-brown filling that Gil knew from his limited experience was delightfully-cappuccino flavored.

"I didn't order no tarbaby *cannoli*."

"Are you sure?" the worker asked. It was a bold move, Gil thought. The worker was young. About his brother's age. Even with the display case and counter in between them, Gil had noticed the spotless red canvas

Chuck Taylor's. New or proud, Gil wasn't sure. New, or proud, it probably didn't matter.

The man didn't take the foolishly-offered bait, though. He just sighed, then:

"*Figlio*, I've been eating *cannoli* for over four decades, and never once during that time have I *ever* wanted a tarbaby one. So, stop the wisecracks, reach back in there, and grab me another traditional, *capiche? Chi cazzo credi di essare?*"

"What do you want me to do with this one?" the clerk said.

"I don't give two flying fucks what you do with it. Stick it up your Aunt Carla's ass, see if she's into that, if you like."

"I'll take it," Boner inexplicably announced himself.

Both the clerk and the man turned and stared at Boner, as if trying to process this alien novelty that materialized into their world. The silence was deafening, broken finally by a chuckle from the man.

"There you go," he said to the clerk. "The kid wants it. Give it to the kid."

Not knowing what else to do, the clerk held up the *cannoli*, an offering to a god no one worshiped. Boner stepped forward and took it.

"There you go, kid. Enjoy," the man said, tousling Boner's hair. "What's your name, *figlio*?"

"Boner," Jaxon replied.

The man turned and looked at Jaxon, the brow furrowed in disappointment. "I wasn't asking you." He then raised an interrogative eye back at Boner.

"Bonaparte."

The man seemed amused by the reply. "Bonaparte what?"

"Bonaparte Jackson."

"Are Mr. and Mrs. Jackson fans of the French?"

"I don't know."

"No," the man tousled Boner's hair again. "We seldom do. The world of our parents is held in permanent opacity to us, right, kid?" He turned to Jaxon. "And you? You're the smart-ass of the group, I see. What's your name?"

"Tony."

"The fuck it is. You ain't a *paisano*."

"How do you know?"

The man answered with a glare that said everything.

"My name's Jaxon."

"Don't fuck with me, kid." The tone became gravelly and significant.

"He's not," Boner said. "His first name's Jaxon. With an 'x.'"

"Fair enough. So, Jaxon with an 'x,' you got a last name?"

"Palinski."

"Thought so. You don't see too many Pollacks up this way. Mostly just us Guineas. Of course, you got the jungle bunnies and the spics, but you have them everywhere. Lots of dinks around here, too, but I suppose that's the university drawing them in. But not a lot of Pollacks. Most of youse are down south, in Jersey. Which means your parents are either intrepid or just too fucking lazy to move. Which is it, kid?"

For the second time this day, Gil placed his hand on Jaxon's arm, shook his head. Not low-hanging fruit this time. The highest.

The man shifted his gaze to Gil, held it, long and appraising, Into the extended silence, the howl of the abattoir explaining itself.

"And you?" he asked.

"Gillian. Gillian Nash."

Gil hated saying his full name aloud, winced at its vocalization into this confined cumulonimbus atmosphere.

Hated his full name like a stain. His mother and his father treated parenting like a lark. Actually gave his older brother "Danger" as a middle name, to make the joke the flesh, proscribing to Stanford a life of daring risk-taking, as they thought.

Boner knew this about Gil, had once tried to cheer him up, reminded him of that kid who showed up in third grade, who disappeared by fourth, named Justin Case; but Boner said nothing this time.

"Sounds like a spy name," the man replied. "You a spy?"

"No, sir."

The man nodded, as if slotting the final puzzle piece in place.

"So you're the leader?"

"We don't have a leader."

"But I'm talking to the right kid?"

Gil let the silence answer. The man nodded again.

"Where you kids headed?"

"To Cutler's," Boner replied.

"To Cutler's," the man repeated, still looking into Gil. "Nice. Me, I prefer classical. Or opera. After a long or a tough day doing what I do, some opera is a nice capper. Takes an edge off." He paused a moment in personal, hermetic reverie. "Of course, for that, you can't get anything better than Beethoven's Ninth. Yeah, I think that's my favorite, what works best, after a day doing what I do. 'Ode to Joy.' Ironic, isn't it?"

"I wouldn't know," Gil said.

"I think you do." Turning back to the clerk, he said, "Whatever these kids want, it's on me. I'll settle up when I come back." He looked once again into Gil. "*Tutto fatto*," he said, nodding his head at the clerk. "I think I just may listen to the Ninth tonight. It's been awhile. Try the *tres leches*, boys. It's divine. Some people," his eyes flashed to Jaxon, then back to Gil, "don't know what *tres leches* means. Think it means, 'three tears.' It doesn't. But it could."

The man turned and walked out of Libby's, back into the pure world of his own creation.

"I'm not waiting in that line," Boner said, pointing at the line of customers in front of world-famous Frank Pepe's.

"You're right, you're not," Gil replied, steering his friends towards a small building recessed in the parking lot adjacent to Pepe's.

It is only the ignorant, the unformed or uninformed palate that goes to New York City for the world's finest pizza. While the fare there is commendable, true initiates know that to get the world's finest pizza, one must travel an additional 80 miles up the eastern coastline. Thin-crusted, coal-fired, Neapolitan in style like its big city brethren, the real secret, what separated New Haven pizza from everything else, as locals knew full well, is the dough, more specifically the water in it, that keeps it slightly chewy despite the charring of the brick ovens. Pepe's is world famous, attracting tourists like moths; Presidents interrupt flyovers to stop at Sally's; the locals know not to sleep on Modern Apizza. But none of the three boys had ever been to this hidden, hole-in-the-wall.

"What is this place," Boner asked with wonder, seated at a table with nary a wait.

"It's called The Spot. My brother told me about," Gil replied.

"I thought we were going to Pepe's."

"Did you see that line? Pepe's is for suckers. Besides, you see that wall? You see those ovens?"

"Yeah."

"Those are Pepe's ovens."

"What?"

"Owned and operated by the same family, share a wall and the ovens. You, my friend, will be eating a fine Pepe's pie, without standing in that line. Like I said, Pepe's is for suckers." As if nervously aware of the sacrilege of such a statement, Gil amended, "I mean, waiting in line to get a table is for suckers."

They ate their slices in silence for a while, treating each bite as a ritual.

Jaxon broke the silence. "You know who that was, don't you?"

"Yeah," Gil said. "I know who that was."

"Who?" Boner asked.

"The guy who bought your *cannoli.*"

"Who was he?"

"George Franccese," Gil said.

"George 'The Lips,'" Jaxon added.

"Who's that?"

"Only the most dangerous mobster in New Haven," Jaxon said.

"Allegedly," Gil added.

"He's a goodfella. A made man, they say."

"The Mafia's in New Haven?" Boner said.

"Are you fucking kidding me?" Jaxon almost spit out his birch beer in stunned surprise. "Are there mobsters in New Haven? Does Father Dougan fuck altar boys?"

"Hey, I was an altar boy," Boner said.

"Well, then, you know the answer, don't you? Do you know why they call him 'The Lips'?"

"No."

"He likes to take them as trophies. I heard he uses them as bait when he goes deep-sea fishing."

"What I heard," Gil said, "is he keeps them all in a freezer. In little baggies, labeled and dated."

"Your brother tell you that?"

"Yeah."

"What does *tutto fatto* mean?" Boner asked.

"I don't know," Gil answered, although he knew what it meant and knew what it meant.

"Do you think the mob had something to do with the bomb threat?" Boner asked, his voice that of a child asking for a scary story.

Gil gave his friend a long, penetrating look, one laced with the forgiveness of the confessor, with the lament of the penitent. "No, Boner. I don't," he said.

"I heard this story about Franccese," Jaxon interrupted, "about his daughter. So, for her prom, she asks this junior she's hot on to take her. They've been friends for a year or so, but he's not interested in anything else, right? But he figures, she's got money, it's a prom, why not? Go have a good time and all. So, he picks her up, and there's Franccese. Tells the kid he wants to have a word with him. Puts his arm around his shoulders and walks him through the garden in the backyard. Tells him, 'I want my daughter to have the time of her life, *capiche?* The time of her life. Anything she wants to do, you do, got it? If she does *not* have the time of her life, you and I are going to have another talk. Trust me, kid; you *don't* want to have that other talk.'

So, guy's scared shitless. I mean, who wouldn't be? But they go to the prom, they dance, they drink a little. They drink a little more. Guy comes to find out she's booked a room at the hotel where they're having the prom. Tells him she wants him to take her up to the room and fuck her silly.

He doesn't know what to do. He doesn't think of her that way. Not attracted to her at all, because she's like this heavy Italian chick right? Mustache and everything. And 'roll her in dough and aim for the wet spot' kinda big. He's afraid if he fucks her, he's stuck dating her, and how do you ever break up with a mobster's daughter? At the same time, Franccese said to do whatever she wants. And this is what she wants. Long story short,"

"Too late," Boner joked.

"Eat a bag of dicks! I'm telling a story here."

"So tell it."

"Long story short, he fucks her. And when word of it gets back to Franccese, because somehow, word of it gets back to Franccese, he has the guy whacked for fucking his daughter. Ain't that a pisser? Franccese tells this guy 'do what she wants or I'll kill you,' guy does what she wants, Franccese kills him anyway."

"That's why I'm not having anything to do with girls," Boner said.

Jaxon gave him the exaggerated once-over again, rolled his eyes. "Yeah," he said, "that's why."

"I heard the family just moved away," Gil said.

"Your brother tell you that?" Jaxon mocked.

"Yeah, he did."

"He tell you when to jerk-off, too?"

"No, your mother still does that."

It was reflexive, the traditional testosterone-laden verbal joust of boys who are not yet men. He said it without thinking, but still it contained in its core the seed of all wars, of genocide and "cleansings." Gil knew that once the arrow had been fired, it could not be recalled; it must find its mark, must deliver its sting, must piece the heart. The heart requires such things, for reasons we no longer fathom, rituals cauterized into our collective scar.

"Oh, Jaxon, man, I am so sorry."

Nothing else could be offered, for nothing else could now be ventured, the rupture no longer his to repair.

By the set of his friend's jaw, Gil knew he felt the wound quick and deep, but that he also understood his part in the ritual, the one that called for festering, that offered only two choices: bitterness or, paltry by its side, forgiveness and brotherhood.

"Don't worry about it," Jaxon said, standing and throwing a $5 bill on the table as tip, a performative generosity that kept his choice, like all such choices, veiled.

A crowd has gathered in the asphalt pathway between Pepe's and Libby's, jarred loose from their mundane routine by yellow tape, blue and red lights flashing. Except for the tape and the lights, the world had gone colorless, shades of gray: store front, concrete, pathways and road; dry gray, wet gray, light gray, dark gray. Everything gray, excepting the yellow tape, the blue and red lights flashing, and, protruding out of the Dumpster behind Libby's, spotless red canvas Chuck Taylor's. New or proud, Gil wasn't sure.

Holy shit," Boner cried out. "Isn't that the—"

Gil winced, shut his eyes, knowing that worlds had just been exchanged.

"Shut your mouth, Boner," Jaxon hissed.

But it was too late. The cop closest to them, the one half-heartedly doing crowd-control on a half-hearted crowd, had heard.

"You know something, kid?"

"Yeah, we were just here, about thirty minutes ago. He got us our *cannoli*."

They were led under the tape, away from the crowd, and brought before a detective, question laden, like a blood-hound waiting for a glove. Pad and pen in hand, he began, asking his questions. And the glove, as if performing the role of a lifetime, gave his dutiful answers.

The tectonic shift of each question, each answer now beyond Gil's control. He could no longer stop it, could no longer save his friend. He could only watch and hope, hope that a name would not be mentioned. And if it was?

Well, then Gil would have nothing to offer beyond the paltry aid of commiseration.

The name flittered and floated out of reach of the first half-dozen questions, giving Gil the burning cruelty of hope. But then he heard it, gliding, with the blithe confidence of Icarus, over the susurrus of the crowd,

"Yeah. George Franccese. He bought us *cannoli*."

"Stupid mother-fucker," Jaxon mumbled the curse beside Gil.

"Do you know why they call him 'The Lips?'" Boner beamed his question.

But the detective did not want to know. The detective, surely, already knew. But the detective was certainly hooked, his face that of the euphoric puzzle-finisher, serendipitously handed the missing last piece.

"Thanks, kid," he said, tapping Boner on the head with his flip-closed notepad, into which he had already scribbled Boner's name and address. He tousled the kid's hair to complete the symmetry.

"Where you kids headed?" he added, addressing all of them for the first time.

His question-answering momentum unchecked, Boner replied, "Cutler's"

"Ah, buying some music, huh? Well, for my money, nothing beats classic rock. Something like The Band, you know? Something with a somber beat, poignant lyrics, you know? Like 'The Weight' or 'Stage Fright' or 'The Night They Drove Old Dixie Down.' Those are some *real* songs. Check them out, boys." He tapped Boner on the head with the notepad one last time, for luck, of consequence dubious.

Boner nodded the nod of the prize-pupil, just graced with a perfect score. Jaxon and Gil said nothing. There was nothing to say. And, the Point-of-No-Return now irrecoverably past, there was nothing else to do but resume their journey.

***

In Wooster Square Park, man-creatures slept under benches, enfolded within layers of discarded jackets and frayed blankets, their soiled coats the corpses of the free market, the promise of capitalism lined inside lint-frayed pockets, cardboard beds slowing the seepage of wet earth and insect horde. They will arise in the dark, scouring through the leavings, fostered by detritus, scrap-nourished, but for now, they sleep. Some dream, faint memories of hot water and tables; some will chase those dreams away with cheap bottled wine when the night comes; some are hollow, scoured free of dream and memory. They will arise in the dark, writhe and shuffle, moaning the long, unheard dirge of a collective, harrowed soul.

But for now, they sleep. And amongst them walks a man, bone-thin and pale, his eyes hidden under the brim of an anachronistic top hat, feeding on this atmosphere of despair. He has been to Libby's already; has whispered of disrespect in an ear beneath pomaded hair the black of the universe. St. Christopher amuses him. He has stood in line at Pepe's. In due time, he will be elsewhere. In due time, he will be everywhere. He whistles. The blown fluctuations of someone who is not good at it, but thinks he is, although the occasional self-denigrating grin suggests he probably knows the truth.

But the tune, and whether it is melodic or not, is in harmony with the scene, or with the hopes and dreams and memories surrounding, does not matter. It never has.

And he is once again, as always, prowling, interminable.

They had walked several blocks in silence, past the depressing humanity of Wooster Square Park, down Chapel again, along the New Haven Green, where Gil's brother would spend summer Saturday nights, ostensibly listening to bands like Spyro Gyra, but really just folding himself into the mass public drunkenness, no IDs checked because no IDs possible.

They walked on in silence.

Beyond the Green, the crumbled facade of an old civilization. A derelict downtown mall, once every bit the Mecca as Cutler's. A decrepit building that once claimed the grandiose label, "The New Haven Coliseum." Gil's brother had gone to several concerts there, a timeline kept in black T-shirts. Judas Priest, Iron Maiden, Ronnie James Dio. His last concert, The Beastie Boys. So disgusted by the crumbling facilities that they did a one-song encore, an ad lib they titled, "Fuck New Haven." No need, Mike D. Someone beat you to it.

Gil's father used to drop him off there to watch the New Haven Nighthawks play, before the franchise renamed, then relocated itself.

"I feel that every year, there's a new hottest pepper. You ever notice that?" Boner broke the calcified silence.

Jaxon pounced, predator staking out the watering hole.

"You stupid, fat, fuck-face! What the fuck were you thinking?"

"I was thinking about hot peppers, duh. What's gotten into you?"

"What's gotten into me?!? What's gotten into me? What were you thinking, talking to that cop?"

"Why wouldn't I talk to the cop?"

"My God, you are too stupid to live. Which is good, because you're not going to. Do I have to spell it out to you? You *named* George Franccese. *And* you gave that cop your name and your address."

"So?"

"So?!? So?!? So, what do you think Franccese is going to do to you, you fat fuck? He's going to have you killed. If he doesn't do it himself, that is. He's going to kill you. He's going to cut off your lips and then feed them to a tuna. And probably kill your entire family. And probably us too, for being dumb enough to be your friends. You stupid fat fucking retard!"

Gil said nothing. He knew Jaxon's anger at Boner, for it was his as well. But he also knew that Jaxon's rage contained more. It contained his mother walking out; it contained his father's alcoholism; it contained all the pain and doubt and fear that made Jaxon who he was, that was his blanket. All laced into this attack, as if Jaxon had conflated his friend with the idea of redemption, as if he thought that somehow if he could keep Boner safe, all that was his would be corrected, his mother returned, his father sober, all right with the world again. But now Boner, through an instinctive and neophyte naiveté, had called down the thunder upon his own head. And in doing so, had deprived Jaxon of his last illusion.

And so Jaxon cursed and yelled, his avalanche anger devolving into mere vocalization by the end, words replaced with atavistic howls of pain and rage.

"Boys," a voice called from behind them, "what's with all this racket?"

An old, weathered and wrinkled black man, garbed in the uniform of the disenfranchised and dishomed, shuffled out of an alley, a smile, bright and resplendent unfolded beneath his vacant and wandering empty eyes.

"What's all this about?" he repeated.

"Nothing," Jaxon said. "We were just talking."

"Don't sound like they's was much talking about it. Beginning was just a bunch a words you boys shouldn't be using, and the end there, sounded like an old catamount caught his leg in trap. That the case, boy," he addressed Jaxon, "you got your leg in a trap, can't see no way to get it out?"

"No. What the fuck you know about it, anyway, old man?"

The man sighed, through his lungs the disappointed wind of the world, the powerless breeze bouncing off those who refused to see.

"There you go again. They's words you shouldn't be using yet. Time enough to use them later. Maybe sooner than you think, sooner than I'd like to think on, anyway. Now, I may be old, and I may be blind, but there's still some dregs left in this old barrel. So let me give you some advice, son. What's coming is coming. Does no good to howl at the trap or wonder how you got in it." Turning now to Boner, "And it does no good to make love to the trap either. Won't make it go any smoother, if that's what you're after. The trap is the trap. It's gonna do what it's gonna do, when it's time to do it. *You* know what I'm talking about," he said, turning his slate-gray eyes now to Gil. "You know what's coming, what's always been coming. There's been some days, you even heard some of its footsteps, if'n I'm guessing right."

Gil, his mouth and throat gone dry, only nodded.

"Headed toward that record store, I reckon?"

Again, Gil, surprised by his unsurprise, just nodded.

"They's lot of music in that store. Whole lots of music. Of all different kinds. Course, what I prefer is jazz. They play some over on that Green in the summer, some days. I sure do like to listen to it. Life is jazz, son. Like your friends here. They jazz too. You don't need no record store for that. Why don't you boys go on home? Leave the store for some other day, some other person. Go on home. Be safe from the words for a little while longer. They find you soon enough as it is. Go on home."

They did not go home. There is never really the option to go home, just to go on.

They walked several blocks more, in a different kind of silence this time, past restaurants from Tibet and Ethiopia, past subterranean galleries, past ivy-covered walls. Behind them, around them, a whistling, off-key and disharmonic, echoing through the grime and slime muck covered alleys past which they continued their march.

When they got to Cutler's, they split, each looking for whatever they felt justified themselves.

Before parting, Jaxon whispered in Gil's ear, "And I know you think I called in that bomb threat, so fuck you too!" He walked off into the fading halo of childhood. Gil watched him grab albums with covers that illustrated the gossamer limits of a soul irrevocably sundered.

Boner wandered the aisles, mumbling, "So many choices; too many choices" to himself over and again.

Gil, overwhelmed suddenly with a feeling of full, encompassing futility, went to wait outside, no longer driven by the desire to search, no longer with the need to find what was in all probability misplaced, or which was never there to begin with.

She was tired from an overly-randy late-morning rush. Three customers a day was solid earning; three in the stretch when most are thinking about, enjoying, then recalling lunch was a noteworthy anomaly. Followed by another anomaly, to put it mildly. The pale, thin man didn't want the usual tricks. He wanted her to lure one of them—"It doesn't matter which," he said. "I got nothing but time"—up to the room, where he was waiting. He was paying in a currency she could not refuse. The promise of more time, of a slowing down, a reversing of the taint flowing inexorably through her veins; the promise of more time. She would slit a throat for more time. But he wasn't asking her to do that. He was asking for something much simpler, easier, and laden with plausible deniability. He wanted her to lure one of them. It didn't matter which. And he was paying in a currency she could not refuse.

Gil was side-gazing her well before she approached. She was hard not to notice. Cleavage straining against lace, tanned legs calling down additional tribute from the sun, lipstick good for only one thing, boxed flaxen hair. But what held his attention, what called down the stirrings, the engorgement, were the snakes. Tattooed down her arms, up her legs, tapering like a directive arrow, pointing towards mounds of promise. His mouth was long dry before she spoke.

"You out here all alone?"

"My friends are inside."

"Music lovers, huh?

"Yeah."

"But not you?"

"No. I mean, yeah. I mean, just not right now"

She smiled. "You should go get yourself a nice love song in there, baby. All kinds of love songs in there. Play them for your girlfriend."

She then purred, "Lots of love songs out here, too. You can play those for your girlfriend as well. Once you learn the moves." She nodded toward the awning from under which she first emerged. "Do you wanna come inside, baby? Learn some moves?"

The hairs along the back of his neck screamed this was not what he wanted despite it being everything he wanted. He swallowed, tasting the harsh bile of regret, the lingering salty sting of not yet.

"I do," he said, "but I better not. My friends."

She looked at him, hard at first, the hardness of time promised falling away, then softer, a something she thought long buried and gone reasserting itself in these final moments—for while it was not expressed, she instinctively felt the price for returning to the room empty-handed, the price of sacrifice, was more than she had left to pay, and then felt she'd pay it anyway.

"I suppose you're right, baby. There'll be plenty of time for that. No need to do it just yet. It'll come, soon enough."

Later that night, Gil will lie in his room, under the dark of night, under the heavy clarity of unannounced revelation. His epiphanies will be legion.

He knows that Boner called in the bomb threat, and he knows why. His desperate need to be noticed, to create some movement in the world at his own behest. To make something, anything, happen.

He knows Jaxon's mom will never return, is already comfortably ensconced in another's arms, in another's orbit, and gives only fleeting thought to what was left behind.

He knows that George Franccese is an icon, worshiped by all, revered by none, whose presence is a requirement of the system, created by our collective frustrated aspirations.

Gil knows there will be a day he will go by Gillian, will not remember schoolmates, or will make them into hazy amalgams. He would like to talk to Boner or to Jaxon then, he supposed, but felt they would not be around anymore, or, if they were, they would be just the faintest shadows of who they are now, broken for different reasons and by different weights.

He knows that Boner is too good for this world. He won't make it. If Franccese doesn't get him, something else will. As it will get Jaxon, too.

He knows that he will think back on this trip, will wish he'd made it more often, all the while understanding that if he did, he would no longer wish this. He will make this trip into myth. Myth is often made up of such mundane things.

He didn't buy any music. No jazz, no Beethoven's Ninth, no classic rock, no love song. There was no point.

Nor did he buy the record his brother paid him for. His brother could buy it himself, could make his own trip.

The whole idea was foolish. Cutler's was just a store.

The blind man was right; there is music everywhere in the world. Hymns of religious randomness, of which we are acolytes all, parishioners none. Empty psalms in endless search for a harmony that shall never come. An off-key whistling that dogs our steps, until it finds and claims us.

As if Place Matters

On April 11, 1981, twenty-five hundred miles away from Edmonton, Alberta—where Wayne Gretzky would record his first career playoff hat trick in a 6-2 win against Montreal, a win that would wrap up a shocking sweep of the heavily-favored Canadians—in the quiet suburban town of North Bainbridge, Connecticut—a town where hockey was not a religion, not quite a ceremony, but something more than a pastime or a hobby, something lodged at the level of, say, a ritual—Johnny Eglend (who was just starting to recognize the faint sense of an idea that he would soon prefer to be called "John") was sitting on the roof of the defunct Montowese Elementary School, talking to his best friend, Richard, unaware that he had only a few hours of conscious life left to him, while, below them, more than a dozen of their other friends, with whom they shared varying levels of intimacy, ran around in the dark, playing "War", a game—requiring, as it did, the use of cheap, plastic guns one buys in toys stores and imaginary (and thoroughly, argumentatively inconclusive) "shootings"— (in fact, the plaintive whining of "I shot you" from Tommy Tubblefield—all 210 bloated pounds of him— drifted up to Johnny and Richard from a field on the other side of the school's gymnasium)—they were far too old to still be playing (and they were all just a little too young to be playing a similar game for real) (Johnny's father, incidentally, was at home drinking the first of what would be several Jack and Cokes, watching his favorite hockey team—the New York Rangers—pull off their own playoff surprise—scoring 10 goals against the favored Los Angeles Kings (although the Rangers would have to wait until the next day, April 12, to finish off the playoff series, 3 games to 1—a game Johnny's father rushed back from the hospital to record; a fan to the end, Johnny's father couldn't miss the close-out win—after all, who knew how long a coma could last?))—when Joe Esperi—the soon-to-be-anointed QB savior for the long-suffering North Bainbridge High football fans—frustrated by Tommy Tubblefield's whining and of Marc Fizer's ninja-like shadowy waftings, popping out time and again to definitively (although--according to the rules of the game—temporarily) eliminate Joe from the game (and weary of the daily beatings Joe's father gave him for "not working out hard enough"—for Joe's father, like Johnny's (although in a different sport) had long-since decided his son's football stardom was his meal-ticket out of debt and anonymity, although no one playing "War" at the defunct Montowese Elementary School that night—nor the two friends sitting out the game on the roof talking, one of them not aware that he had only a few hours of conscious life left to him—knew that about Joe), called up at Johnny and Richard, "What they fuck are you guys doing up there? We said that's against the rules. You guys are cheating!"

"We're not playing anymore," Richard explained.

"So the rules don't apply," Johnny added. Ill-advisedly, as it turned out.

Because it was night, and the lights at the defunct Montowese Elementary School were no longer turned on, neither boy on the roof could see the seething face of Joe Esperi, a face of someone who had had *exactly* enough.

"Come down here," he said in a tightly-controlled voice. "so we can talk about it. I don't feel like shouting."

Since the request was both reasonable and easy to satisfy, the two boys, one of them with even fewer moments of conscious life left him, complied.

Once the two boys had climbed down from the roof and walked over to where Joe Esperi stood in the parking lot—fuming silently—although neither Richard nor Johnny could see this in the darkness of the disconnected lighting of the defunct Montowese Elementary School—Joe pounced.

He pushed. He jabbed with his finger. And he shouted. It was the shouting that, ironically for someone so upset the integrity, the sanctity, of the game had somehow—explicable only to him—been sullied, brought the game to a halt, the other players assembling, as if obligated by ritual (but not quite ceremony) around the fuming Joe and the confused Richard and Johnny. Very early in his ranting, he exceeded what would seem a reasonable (although still excessive) level of anger for the perceived (although far from acknowledged) crime of Richard and Johnny.

Richard was smart enough to stay silent this whole time, waiting until the storm passed, until the wave crested over and receded. Johnny also stayed this smart, this silent. For as long as he could. Which, unfortunately (for someone with so few moments of conscious life left him) was not long enough.

Before the wave could crest, he shouted into it:

"We weren't cheating, for fuck's sake. We didn't want to play anymore. So, as I said, the rules didn't apply. It's not a big fucking deal?"

Joe, for whom rules *always* applied, whose father made sure—daily—he understood that, thought this *was* a big fucking deal. And so, he decided to explain that to Johnny.

But not with words. At first, he explained with a lumbering—for Joe was an avid weight-lifter, one of the many reasons the long-suffering fans of North Bainbridge High football held such hope—charge, a charge that during many of the life-times assembled around the three boys in the parking lot of the defunct Montowese Elementary School would subconsciously be remembered whenever one of them saw footage of a rhinoceros running (which happens surprisingly often to those who grow up and who live in quiet suburban towns like North Bainbridge, Connecticut). Joe Esperi, who gave the long-suffering fans North Bainbridge High football such hope, then explained it with a leg, thrust behind the legs of Johnny Eglend, a leg that formed a hypotenuse with the stocky, just-recently lumbering, weight-lifting body of Joe Esperi and the asphalt of the parking lot of the defunct Montowese Elementary School. Finally, he explained it with a violent shove, which, because of the leg that formed a hypotenuse with the stocky, just-recently lumbering, weight-lifting body of Joe Esperi and the asphalt of the parking lot of the defunct Montowese Elementary School, thrust Johnny Eglend backwards.

If all of Joe's explaining had taken place a few inches closer to the edge of the parking lot of the defunct Montowese Elementary School, Johnny's head would have landed in the beginning inches of a soft, grassy field—one that was plush with plant, as it was only rarely mowed by the town's Park and Recreation workers. As if place matters.

At the 15:54 mark of the first period, Gretzky, 20—only five years older than Johnny Eglend—which may have been part of the problem—set up shop behind the Canadians' goal, a chunk of ice from which Gretzky would set up so many goals for teammates throughout his career, it came to be called his "office," made a crisp, sharp, pass up the ice to defenseman Paul Coffey—himself a future Hall of Famer. Coffey's shot from the point beat a screened Richard Sevigny, putting the Oilers on top 2-0. The assist, an appetizer—or, since this story, at least in some small part, involves the Montreal Canadians—an *hors d'oeuvres*, to Gretzky's noteworthy goal-scoring achievement, occurred just as Johnny Eglend's head hit the asphalt of the defunct Montowese Elementary School parking lot.

***

Four years earlier, when Johnny was just an 11-year-old a few years into his hockey career, long before any of the fans of North Bainbridge High hockey would begin to form hope, long before Johnny's father began—like Joe Esperi's father, to see his son as his meal-ticket out of debt and anonymity, the goaltender on Johnny's team, Tommy Tubblefield—chosen solely on the size and shape of his bloated body--came down with the flu, began vomiting in between the first and second periods of a game. Desperately-pressed, the coach asked for a volunteer to step in, finish the game in net. Johnny, who, unlike his father, recognized he was not a very talented forward, talented enough to play for a few more years—although, as this story has already made clear, that proved to be the case in any event, for reasons that had little to do with talent, unless one considers the talent Joe Esperi's leg had being a hypotenuse with the stocky, just-recently lumbering, weight-lifting body of Joe Esperi and the asphalt of the parking lot of the defunct Montowese Elementary School or the talent Joe Esperi had in shoving someone over the leg being a hypotenuse with the stocky, just-recently lumbering, weight-lifting body of Joe Esperi and the asphalt of the parking lot of the defunct Montowese Elementary School—volunteered to take one for the team (which, incidentally, was the phrase Joe Esperi's father would use when trying to encourage his son to work out with the intensity needed to get the stocky, lumbering, weight-lifting body that gave the long-suffering fans of North Bainbridge High football such hope). Tommy Tubblefield would never see the ice again, would have a great view from the bench, as Johnny began a career in net that, while not necessarily widely-known—for hockey in the quiet suburban town of North Bainbridge, Connecticut was not a religion, not quite a ceremony, but something more than a pastime or a hobby, something lodged at the level of, say, a ritual—did give the fans of North Bainbridge High hockey such hope.

Two years into this hope-giving start to a career, Johnny Eglend came into the room where his father was watching TV, crying.

Annoyed (or perhaps—although there is plenty of evidence—some of it contained in this story—to suggest otherwise—genuinely concerned), Johnny's father asked him what was wrong.

"Pelle Lindbergh is dead," Johnny sobbed out with difficulty. Ill-advisedly, as it turned out.

Pelle Lindbergh was a young NHL goalie, one with great promise, who gave many fans a great sense of hope. Since Johnny's father was in the early stages of thinking his son, just maybe, could be his meal-ticket out of debt and anonymity (although he had not yet, and incidentally, never would, quite reach the level of the father of Joe Esperi), one would think he would embrace his son's idolization of Pelle Lindbergh, would celebrate his son adopting many of Lindbergh's mannerisms on the ice (instead of threatening Johnny with punishments if he did not "knock it off"), but, as may have been mentioned already—but in a parenthetical, which is not only apt to be glossed over, but where writers sometimes put information that can be (at the very least) disconcerting—Johnny's father was a hopeful (perhaps overly, perhaps even dysfunctionally, with a faint whiff of dangerous neurosis mixed in with it) fan of the New York Rangers (who would score ten goals on the last night of Johnny's conscious life, and whose series-clinching game the next day his father would record, despite Johnny's coma).

Pelle Lindbergh played goalie for the Philadelphia Flyers—not just Johnny's favorite team, but the bitter, hated rival of the New York Rangers and, by extension, of Johnny's father.

(Someone, somewhere reading this will wonder if Pelle Lindbergh died two years before Johnny Eglend, as this story suggests, or in 1985, as a quick Google search would suggest. As if dates mattered).

"Good," Johnny's father said (for the news, while objectively tragic, was such to give fans—or at least fans with a certain mentality, which, if it has not already been established, will be throughout the course of the story, Johnny's father unquestionable had—a sense of hope).

Perhaps because Johnny's best friend Richard was so good at letting the storm pass over, letting the wave crest and recede (or perhaps because his grief was so comprehensive he did not immediately process what his father said), Johnny explained how Pelle Lindbergh, who gave Philadelphia Flyers fans such hope, had died.

"He died in a car crash," he said. "The news said he 'failed to negotiate a curve.'"

"All that means is he was going too fast," his father sneered. Never having had an idol himself, Johnny's father did not understand how his son was feeling.

"He was probably drunk," he added.

Incidentally, in interview after interview, when asked about who his own idols were, Wayne Gretzky would frequently mention (not surprisingly) Gordie Howe. He would also always mention his father.

At the 8:15 mark of the second period, Gretzky would take a soft saucer pass from center Brett Callighen and deposit it in the Canadians net, with the distracted smoothness of one shooing away a mildly noisome fly. The second assist, incidentally, went to defenseman Paul Coffey, himself a future Hall of Famer.

At the time of Gretzky's first goal, the New York Rangers led the Los Angeles Kings, 8-2, much to the Jack-and-Coke-addled delight of Johnny's father.

At the time of Gretzky's first goal, Richard and a few other friends, Joe Esperi (perhaps surprisingly) among them, brought Johnny Eglend into the front room of his house. This was once the garage, but had been converted to a rec room after it became clear to Johnny's father that his son was a fan (of wavering degrees of hopefulness) of teams that were the bitter rivals of his own. When the Flyers played the Rangers, or the Phillies played the Mets, the father and the son watched these games in separate rooms. When his team was not doing well, Johnny's father often locked the door connecting the rec room with the house proper. He did this because he did not want to hear his son gloat (because that is what he would—and frequently did—do in his son's position). The fact that Johnny never gloated did not (like so many things don't) matter.

Johnny Eglend had regained, (briefly, as it would turn out) consciousness in the car, but now was noticeably dizzy and unbalanced. His speech was groggy and confused. His friends (which included Joe Esperi, who gave fans of North Bainbridge High football such hope) set Johnny on the couch. Richard went to talk to Johnny's father, to explain what happened. It was unclear if Johnny's father was listening, for Mike Allison just scored for the Rangers, putting them up 9-2 now.

Richard was about to repeat the story when Johnny's father waved him off (for some people, nothing is more annoying than a story that repeats).

"Yeah, I got it," Johnny's father said. "Don't worry about him. I'll let him sleep it off. He'll be fine."

The CDC recommends the following treatment for concussions: rest, in short intervals. It is important, the CDC indicates, that rest periods last 30-60 minutes. Particularly with children, it is important to occasionally wake the concussed patient, to ensure that they can be roused. While rest is a vital component to recovery from a brain injury like a concussion, it is also important to monitor the patient, to ensure that the injury is not more serious than it may appear.

For years upon years, many people (including Joe Esperi) who knew the story about Johnny Eglend, April 11, and the parking lot of the defunct Montowese Elementary School, believed that Joe Esperi was responsible for the death of Johnny Eglend.

Three years after Johnny Eglend, now a freshman, replaced Tommy Tubblefield in net, things began to happen. Johnny's father began to think more frequently of his son as a meal-ticket out of debt and anonymity (although even now, not as frequently as Joe Esperi's father did). And fans of North Bainbridge High hockey began to have hope, real hope.

One of the games that crystalized such feelings of hope was (surprisingly) a 7-0 drubbing at the hands of East Catholic. East Catholic was one of the powerhouse programs in the state (if Connecticut, a state where hockey was not a religion, not quite a ceremony, but something more than a pastime or a hobby, something lodged at the level of, say, a ritual, can be said to have powerhouse programs). And while a goalie giving up seven goals seems an unlikely breakthrough moment, a look at the box score would provide some context. That night, Johnny Eglend faced 71 shots, meaning he made 64 saves, many of them spectacular. If an average goalie was in net for North Bainbridge that night, East Catholic may have scored twenty goals (which would have set a state record, eclipsing the eighteen goals Cheshire once scored on

Lyman Hall). The one thing that game made clear (other than that East Catholic was a powerhouse program, at least by Connecticut standards) was that Johnny Eglend was not average; that he may, in fact, be something else.

That was clear to the North Bainbridge coach, who suspended the alternate-start system he instilled for Johnny Eglend and Peter Northinggate, a senior goaltender who people often said "put in his time" and "took one for the team" over the three years he played for North Bainbridge. From the East Catholic game on, Johnny Eglend was the one and only starter.

It was clear to Cunningham Carter, the improbably-named coach of East Catholic, who, when he left East Catholic after the 1981 season to take over at The Gunnery, a prep school with a habit of producing NHL prospects, he thought about that young goaltender from North Bainbridge (what was his name?), thought about tracking him down and offering him a spot on the team (Much like Cunningham Carter cannot be held accountable for his improbable name, he also cannot be held accountable for not knowing that Johnny Eglend, who had once given fans of North Bainbridge High hockey such hope, had slipped into a coma and then a short while after, died—not, as perhaps may be surmised, because Johnny's father decided to pull the plug before the Rangers' next series (against the St. Louis Blues—a series the Rangers, much to the delight of the father of Johnny Eglend, would also, surprisingly, win) but because brain injuries are mercurial things—months before Coach Cunningham Carter had the thought about making such an offer).

It was clear to the fans of East Catholic, who, after berating Johnny Eglend mercilessly with the most vile taunts and chants imaginable throughout the game, serenaded him during the game's final moments with the following, heartfelt and earnest, saluting chant:

*"Three cheers for the goalie, for the goalie, for the
goalie*

*Three cheers for the goalie, 'cause he's had a rough
night."*

Johnny Eglend enjoyed hearing that chant. He found it
humorous, and in keeping with his deeply-held conviction
that games are meant to be fun. Even if you face 71 shots.
Even if you are too old to be playing them. Even if
someone else decides they don't want to play anymore, that
they'd rather sit on a rooftop of the defunct Montowese
Elementary School and talk to their best friend. Which is
one reason (albeit far and away the biggest one) why he
was so confused (until, unfortunately, he became a bit
snippy about it) by Joe Esperi's reaction.

(Someone, somewhere reading this will wonder if it
was really Lyman Hall Cheshire scored 18 goals on and
not, say, Torrington, or Enrico Fermi High. As if facts
mattered).

The one person Johnny Eglend's not-average status
wasn't clear to (or, to be more precise, it was clear enough
to reinforce the idea that Johnny might be his meal ticket
out of debt and anonymity, but not clear enough to supplant
a level of anger exceeding what would seem a reasonable
(although still excessive) response to a perceived (although
far from acknowledged) crime)). Johnny's father felt that
the integrity, the sanctity, of the game had
somehow—explicable only to him—been sullied. And that
Johnny had done the sullying.

When his son returned from the game, his father
met him in the rec room (door to the house proper currently
unlocked), with a seething face, the face of someone who
had had *exactly* enough.

"What the fuck were you doing out there?" he asked
in a tightly-controlled voice.

"What do you mean?"

"You know *damn well* what I mean."

"No. I don't." (for Johnny Eglend truly did not).

"All that playing up to the crowd bullshit. *That's* what I mean."

Johnny Eglend had indeed been playing up to the East Catholic crowd. During stoppages, waving their insults on, suggesting he found them fun (which he did). After making a save and freezing the puck, he'd skate over to the glass and show it to them, shrugging his shoulder as if to say, "Did I do that?"

The few North Bainbridge fans who made the drive up to East Catholic—for it was, by Connecticut standards, a long, tedious drive—saw this as evidence that Eglend was delightfully-unflappable, yet another trait which made him a source of such hope.

"I was having fun," Johnny said, unflappingly.

"*Fun*!?!" his father was incredulous. "You find losing 7-0 fun?"

"No. I find the game fun."

"You *embarrassed* me. Do you think embarrassing me is fun?"

Johnny stayed smart, stayed silent. For as long as he could. Which, unfortunately (for someone who genuinely enjoyed having fun) was not long enough.

"Did *you* let in the seven goals? No. What's the big fucking deal?" he said. Ill-advisedly as it turned out.

Johnny's father then did something Joe Esperi's father would understand. He hit Johnny. Hard. Closed-fist hard. And Johnny fell back and (even though there was no leg acting as a hypotenuse with a stocky, lumbering, body and the asphalt of the parking lot of the defunct Montowese Elementary School) down, hitting his head on the tile that made up the pathway through the rec room to the door leading to the house proper, a door which was sometimes (explicable only to Johnny's father) locked.

***

The CDC has this to say about concussions: most concussions are mild and a patient will recover after a few hours or days of rest. However, repeated concussions can cause lasting damage, sometimes resulting in more serious issues, up to and including death.

Incidentally, there is no record of any moment when Wayne Gretzky's father was embarrassed by his son.

Gretzky scored his second goal of that April 11 night at the 18:56 mark of the second period. A balletic breakaway goal so effortlessly executed that it seemed a fair question whether there was even a goalie in the net.

Interestingly, at the same 18:56 mark (although in the *third* period of that game) defenseman Larry Murphy, himself a future Hall of Famer, scored a meaningless goal for the Los Angeles Kings. A goal which Johnny's father felt sullied somehow—explicable only to him—the sanctity of the Rangers' win.

To address this dissatisfaction, he went into the kitchen to mix one last Jack and Coke. Although he was only one room away (and the door was at this moment unlocked), he did not check on Johnny, did not wake his son to ensure he could be roused, did not monitor the patient, to ensure that the injury was not more serious than it appeared.

He did not do these things because he did not believe Richard. He assumed his son's friend was covering for Johnny. He remembered what boys did on weekend nights. So, he did not think his son had a concussion.

"He's probably drunk," he thought to himself.

***

A few months earlier, as the winter of 1981 gathered force for one last yawp, when Connecticut nestled under layers of snow, its fields and forests postcard perfect, Johnny Eglend had had enough. He stayed smart, stayed silent for a long as he could. But then, he couldn't.

He had chosen hockey because his father had never played. Which meant it was more likely to stay fun. He had grown weary of every game of baseball, every game of football, to be followed by a chalk-board breakdown of what he did wrong, of how he could improve. Every overthrown cutoff man, every missed tackle subjected to analysis, ridicule and scorn. Johnny did not care all that much about what he did wrong; he just enjoyed being out there, on the field, with his friends. Johnny did not care all that much about improving (unless by improving, one—but certainly not his father—meant, "how to have more fun playing"). Baseball and football—much like a future game of "War" played with more than a dozen friends—with whom he shared varying levels of intimacy—at the defunct Montowese Elementary School, stopped being fun. And like that game of "War" played with more than a dozen friends—with whom he shared varying levels of intimacy— at the defunct Montowese Elementary School, where Johnny decided to quit and go up on the roof with his best friend, Richard, and just talk, he decided he would stop playing those games.

But not hockey. Hockey stayed fun. Until it almost didn't. But then, he was able to make it fun again in late February of 1981. His father, growing more convinced by the game that Johnny might be his meal ticket out of debt and anonymity, no longer let the fact that he didn't know what in holy Hell he was talking about stop him from resuming the chalkboard post-game breakdown of what Johnny did wrong, of how Johnny could improve.

Johnny tolerated this (at least, to the best of his ability), for one of the things he always and truly respected about his best friend Richard (although, since, in a few month's time, Johnny will slip into a coma and then a short while after, die, which many people (including Joe Esperi) who knew the story about Johnny Eglend, April 11, and the parking lot of the defunct Montowese Elementary School, would blame on Joe Esperi, he would never get the chance to tell Richard this) was his unflappability. Johnny strove to model that, and, to some degree, was reasonably (although not excessively) successful, Richard had an ability to wait until the storm passed, until the wave crested over and receded that Johnny admired.

But one day in late February of 1981, when winter gathered force for one last yawp and Connecticut lay nestled under layers of snow, its fields and forests postcard perfect, Johnny Eglend 's aspired-to unflappability became quite pedestrianly flappable.

"You can't even skate," he said during one of these chalkboard sessions. Ill-advisedly as it turned out.

And because this was incontrovertibly true, it wounded Johnny's father's pride deeply. So deeply, that he was consumed with the need to disprove it. Which brought them to a frozen pond out in the Connecticut countryside in late-February of 1981, where Johnny's father was determined to prove, on the last pellucid ice of winter, that he could, in fact, skate.

(He could not)

(He fell often. And repeatedly)

(Until he gave up, and silently drove home, seething. And dreading to hear his son gloat—because that is what he would—and frequently did—do in his son's position. The fact that Johnny never gloated did not (like so many things don't) matter).

As a result of this late February winter day, two things happened: the chalkboard sessions stopped. And so did something else.

Wayne Gretzky's first playoff hat trick almost did not happen (Well, it most certainly would still have happened, just not during this particular game, which, of course, would throw the whole analogy being so carefully-crafted here, off). After Dave Lomley scored an empty net goal (assisted by defenseman Kevin Lowe, himself a future Hall of Famer) to put the Oilers up 5-2 with less than a minute left in the game, it seemed safe to assume that the scoring was done.

(Someone, somewhere reading this will wonder if was really Dave Lomley who scored the empty net goal. As if names mattered).

But Gretzky's teammates knew he was special, the source of such great hope, would grow to be called "The Great One." And, of course, at only 20 years-old, he was still a kid (within the context of the sport, if nothing else), so they also wanted him to be happy, to have fun. So Garry Lariviere, a journeyman defensemen of no special historical note (beyond the confines of this story) fed Gretzky a pass that he buried into the Canadians net with just seven second left in the game.

As he and his teammates celebrated the goal (and then, seven game seconds later, the series win—an event Johnny's father would have to wait another day (actually two, since he did not watch the taped game until the early hours of his son's second day in the hospital) to see his favorite team enjoy)), Johnny Eglend slipped into a coma he would never come out of.

The second assist on Gretzky's third goal, incidentally, went to defenseman Paul Coffey, himself a future Hall of Famer.

***

In total, Wayne Gretzky would tally ten playoff hat tricks—still, to this day, the most of any player in history. His last one came as a member of the New York Rangers, in 1997, against the Philadelphia Flyers. Sometimes things happen that way.

Many years later, Richard Michaels (it occurs to me that his last name has not yet been mentioned. As if names matter) was enjoying his life as a moderately successful pharmacist. He has a wife; he has two daughters. He has forgotten—not through any spirit of meanness or of disrespect, nor from any need to suppress a traumatic moment from childhood (which, one would have to admit, the death of a best friend, would be), but simply because sometimes things happen that way—much about Johnny Eglend. His one-time best friend has faded to a yearbook photo (which, oddly, Richard can only envision in black and white although he saw it, years ago, in color).

But then one day Richard is sitting in an airport restaurant (a Chili's, if that detail helps) killing a layover on his way to a convention (being held in Chicago—1,638 miles from Edmonton, Alberta) when he catches a glimpse of a hockey game on the TV behind the bar. The Minnesota Wild—a team that did not exist back when Johnny Eglend gave the fans of North Bainbridge High hockey such hope—against the Anaheim Ducks—a team that did not exist back when Johnny Eglend slipped into a coma and then a short while after, died. Although Richard was a fan of the sport growing up, he has not watched a game since 1981 (which, perhaps—although you are free to push the point more strongly—to say, "most certainly," if you wish—is the one lingering acknowledgment of his long dead friend).

Perhaps not surprisingly, seeing the game on the TV makes him think of his friend. He wonders if Johnny would have ever made it to the NHL. Johnny never thought so, and that never seemed to matter to him. That was something Richard always and truly respected about his best friend (although, since Johnny slipped into a coma and then a short while after, died, which many people (including Joe Esperi) who knew the story about Johnny Eglend, April 11, and the parking lot of the defunct Montowese Elementary School, would blame on Joe Esperi, he never got the chance to tell Johnny this) was his ability to do something for the pure fun of it.

(Johnny's father, incidentally, was at his home (no longer in Connecticut) drinking the first of what would be several Jack and Cokes, watching his favorite hockey team—the New York Rangers. He, unlike Richard Michaels, never stopped watching hockey. And every time he does—more so on days when the Rangers do not win—he bemoans his fate. His son, he insists—with every cold, biting sip of whiskey and flat soda—could have made it to the NHL, should have been his meal ticket out of debt and anonymity. If only Johnny had taken it seriously).

In the airport Chili's, Richard continues to wonder. He wonders if Johnny's life would have been different if he didn't live in North Bainbridge, if he had lived, for example, in Edmonton. Or in Montreal. Or even in Chicago.

As if place matters.

<u>LeGrange</u>

1

I was introduced to Cyrus LeGrange years before I met him. Our first encounter was a postcard received when I was thirteen. An image of what seemed to be large floating boulders. A fishing boat in the foreground. The caption on the back identified the scene as Ha Long Bay. Other than that description, and my address printed in a slashing hand that whispered of palsy, there was nothing on the card. No salutation, no commentary, no explanation.

When I showed the card to my mother, she tried to pass it off as some practical joke. Someone having fun with me. But she had no answer for my "Who?" My "why?" didn't fare much better. And she was so masterfully adept at her stylized casualness about the matter that it was only days later that I noted she never handed the card back to me.

Throughout the years that followed, additional postcards would haphazardly appear. Two depicting the Vietnam War Memorial in D.C., one from Cambodia, most from places in Vietnam, with fantastical names like Mỹ Sơn, Mũi Né, and Black Virgin Mountain.

After my experience with the first card, I did not show any of these to my mother. When I was done studying the picture and marveling at the wonder of their unpredictable but steady appearance, I tossed them into a desk drawer and in the miasma of adolescent concerns, they were forgotten. But Cyrus LeGrange would not be put off so casually. He would wait. He would be patient.

During winter break of my senior year in college, my mother told me her cancer had metastasized. I wasn't even aware she *had* cancer.

131

"Well, two packs a day, every day, once your father was gone. Where did you think this was headed?"

I was stung by the hint of intentional self-destruction in the comment. I was stung by the fact she never told me she was sick. And when, a few months later, cancer had finished the job, I was stung by the fact that at the age of twenty-two, I was now an orphan.

A month or so after my brother and I buried our mother, Cyrus LeGrange once again called on my attention.

It came in the form of a box delivered by UPS. The name "LeGrange" scratched in the upper left corner. Inside the box, three tattered black-and-white composition books, with an envelope taped to the top one, my name written on it in the same slashed print of the postcards. Inside was a letter:

Michael,

I'm sorry about your mother. She was a strong woman.

I've wanted to explain myself for so long now. To help you understand. But I don't know the words. My mind fogs, is just a kaleidoscope. I eventually realized the words would never come. These journals from when I still had words will have to do. At the very least, they may provide context. Sometimes, context is all we can ask for.

I spent several minutes re-reading and puzzling over the letter, then moved on to the first journal. I didn't get past the first sentence:

Deployment rumors confirmed. Off to Vietnam. Time for me to answer the call. Like Dad, and Grandpa before him. Time to pony up, for country and freedom.

About the last thing I was in the mood for was testosterone patriotism, that "Rah-rah, for God and Country bullshit." There was more than enough of that in the air already. Country singers fetishizing bomber-strike revenge, courtesy of the 'Ol Stars and Stripes. Cable news networks broadcasting the latest military fireworks display. Tune in tomorrow for the next episode of "Shock and Awe." See your tax dollars at work. Watch buildings blow up in pretty shades of yellow, orange, and blue. Pay no attention to the people inside. I was saturated with it, and in no mood for LeGrange, whoever the hell he was, adding his stale, decades-old, contribution.

I put the journal back in the box it was mailed in, and brought the box out to the garage, adding it to the recycling pile. And in all probability, that's where LeGrange would have stayed if not for my brother.

A few weeks later, trying to remold our relationship as freshly orphaned brothers, I invited myself to his place for a long weekend visit. We sat on couches in his family room on Sunday night, the closing ceremony to what had been a tepidly pleasant stay. During a lull in our scripted, superficial conversation, I glanced out the large picture window, through which Bryan's neighbor's house blazed in holiday lights of red, green, and white.

"Someone likes to get a jump on the holidays," I observed. "Christ, it's only the second week of November."

"He starts earlier every year," Bryan's wife said.

Bryan chuckled. "God, remember Dad would get so fanatical about having the biggest Christmas display in the neighborhood? Had to outdo everyone. 'Bigger and better,' he'd say. But bigger and better wasn't enough. He always wanted to be first too. Remember that year he was out there the day—and I mean *the day*—after Halloween? On his ladder, stapling up as many light strands as he had extension cords to power, and Mom came outside and . . .. Sorry. Sometimes I forget."

"No worries."

I had long-since gotten used to him forgetting that I'm not in any of those stories and have none of my own. I took a long pull at the warmish beer in my hand.

"Do you, by any chance, remember someone named LeGrange?"

Bryan looked like I had just shoved a pineapple up his ass. "Why are you asking?"

Taken aback by the hostility in his voice, I explained briefly about the package, did a fair job paraphrasing the letter and gave my review of the journal based on the one sentence I actually read.

"I have *no* idea what it's all about?" I concluded.

"It's nothing. I hope you threw all that shit away."

"But who is he? And why would he decide to send that to *me*?" Then I remembered the postcards and added those to the story.

"Mom told him to stop sending those," Bryan mumbled into his Scotch, so low that I wasn't sure what I heard.

"But who is he?" I repeated.

"Nobody. Just some crazy guy. Got all fucked up in Vietnam. He's just crazy."

"But I—"

"Just stop! OK? Just fucking stop. LeGrange is just a piece of shit and crazy and just ignore him. Don't have anything to do with him, understand?"

I didn't, and I would have pressed him further had not Jane placed a hand on my arm.

"Please," she said. Her look was pleading. The look of someone who has scouted this path, knows where it leads, doesn't want to travel it again.

I went home and read through the first journal that night:

This jungle air. Goddamn, how I hate this air. So stifling. So thick with wetness. It's like breathing through a sponge.

Every day's the same. We march from some unpronounceable village to another, the names all so foreign, so fantastical. Quang Ngai, Huyen Duc Pho, My Lai.

Jo-Jo keeps asking when do we go to My Tai. Jo-Jo is good at cracking jokes. He can even get Christianson to laugh from time to time.

Jo-Jo even gives it to the Lieutenant. He says he can get away with it because "Here in the 'Nam, the black man can say things to you-alls' white asses that we couldn't say back home. Because we ain't the problem out here. The Yellow Man is. Shit, I sling just a whisper of this jive back home, I got some real problems. Or if'n I were to tell Baker, or Christianson, or your redneck ass to 'go fuck yo momma,'? shit, I'm hanging from a tree. But not here, my man. Not here. Out here, yellow trumps black, you dig?"

Most times, I don't know what the hell Jo-Jo is talking about, but I sure do like to listen to him speak. Grandpa would call him an "uppity nigger" I suppose. He's not like black folk back home. doesn't have that hang-dog look, those dull, sullen eyes. Seems free. And relaxed, if that's even possible in this place. Like most things here, he's not what I expected.

Most of the first journal ran along these lines. A recounting of day-to-day events, populated with people who progressively morphed from mere names on a page to full, round characters. Reading was like watching Polaroid images emerge. That night I was introduced to Jo-Jo from Detroit. He joined the Army because a judge gave him the choice, enlist or jail, after he lifted two packs of cigarettes from a corner store; to Baker, who was about to enroll in the engineering program at Rensselaer Polytechnic Institute when he got his notice. Baker's father offered to drive him up to Montreal, but Baker ultimately decided he had an obligation to go; to Christianson, a thin, quiet, bookish New Englander who, inexplicably, volunteered. His presence there so incongruous, he seemed destined the first to die.

Obviously, the person I most wanted to know was LeGrange, and to that end, the journal was a great disappointment, hardly worth my brother's vehemence. The early pages dripped with enthusiasm wrestling with fear and anxiety. Clichéd phrases like "fighting for my country," "ensuring freedom, here and back home," and "protecting our way of life" abounded.

As I continued to read, patriotism gave way to boredom. LeGrange now complained. About digging fox holes each dusk in unyielding soil, about the inedibility of C-rations, of the "sweltering shithole" of Vietnam. There was nothing new here. I heard all this before, from Oliver Stone, from Michael Herr, from Tim O'Brien. LeGrange's story, such as it was, was told—and told better—already. And not only had I heard this story before, but I was tired of hearing it. I had no interest in another "Vietnam-was-horrible-and-war-sucks" story.

I finished the first journal as a sort of compromise with an earlier self who vowed to read all three, an earlier self who thought he'd find answers there. I thought about throwing the journals into the trash, but a nagging sense that to do so would be a rude gesture stopped me. I placed them back in their box, brought the box back out into the garage, and, for the second time, walked away from Cyrus LeGrange.

2

On last night's ambush, I got my first kill.

That's how the second journal opened. I didn't intend to come across this line and, knowing what I know now, I wish I hadn't. I was cleaning out the garage on an early spring day when I bumped the box containing LeGrange's journals with my elbow, spilling them to the floor. As I picked them up, the cover of the second journal fell open, confronting me with this confession. Siren-called by that line, I sat down on the concrete step bridging the house and garage and read:

On last night's ambush, I got my first kill. The guys have been riding me a little hard about not having one yet.

"Shooting into the jungle don't count," Christianson would always insist. "I'm talking about that intimate moment where there is no doubt a life has been taken and no doubt you're the one that took it."

Jo-Jo got his about three weeks in; Christianson only needed a few days. And Baker? Baker has blown up so many huts, tunnels, and bridges, some of them just for fun, who knows how many he has.

That's what we were talking about last night. Of course, you're not supposed to talk on ambush. You weren't supposed to smoke either, but we were doing that too. And we weren't worried about the LT catching us, losing his shit if he did. We've developed a healthy case of "Fuck the LT" by now. I think he's scared of us anyway. Us. The Four Horsemen. Baker came up with the name. "Where we go, Hell follows." We've discovered we're quite good at this soldiering thing. Not so much the following orders part, but the killing people part. Or at least Jo-Jo, Baker, and Christianson are. I'm not sure why they include me. Christianson says it's because "we see great potential in you."

"How many slopes you think you've lit up so far, Baker?" I asked him.

"Not enough, clearly. Else I'd be in a warm bed, 'stead of in this hole with you."

"No, seriously, Baker. How many you reckon?"

"'You reckon?' Damn, I love the way you Texans talk. Well, I reckon it's hard to say. I've got a different girlfriend than you."

That's what Jo-Jo calls his M-16: his girlfriend. Even gave her a name. Mabel. "Me and Mabel are going out on the town," he'll say before patrol.

"You guys can stroke your barrels all you like," Baker continued. He reached in his rucksack, pulling out a claymore identical to the half dozen we had set up earlier in the night. He rubbed the polished nickel of its concave lovingly. "But this is my pocket pussy."

"What's your point, Baker?"

"My point is that when you blow people up, it's hard to get an accurate count." After a pause, he added, "God, I love this place."

As if on cue, seconds after Baker's declaration of love, claymores farther down the line exploded in sequence. Soon the air was full of sound. As I fired into the shattered jungle, I became aware of movement to my left. Movement—since we were the last team on the horizontal L-line LT set up—that shouldn't be there.

The NVA was unarmed, his gun lost somewhere in the noise. For the first few beats, he just stood there, swaying in harmony to music only he could hear. One of his hands was clamped to the side of his face, the wetness of it glinting in staccato flashes of rifle and claymore.

Our eyes met. We just stared at each other forever. The firefight around us receded into white noise. All that mattered was me and him.

He pulled his hand away from the wound on his head and held it out to me, as if asking me to dance. I took and held it.

Then, as the sounds of chaos resumed, I jerked him off his feet into the depression Baker and I had carved into the slant of the hill.

Up close I could see that the head wound was not serious. A part of his ear gone. Needed some basic field care and he'd be fine.

I slipped the combat knife from my belt and gently, softly pushed it into his stomach. His body tensed, a low moan. I slid the blade in and out of the wound, slowly at first, then gradually faster, penetrating deeper with each thrust. At some point, a cease-fire was called, although I did not hear it. My back arched with one final, deep thrust and I held it, savoring the moment. I let my gaze wander over him, absorbing every detail, the trails beads of sweat took as they coursed down his cheeks, the three stray strands of hair matted on his forehead, the way the fingers on his right hand were bent in the "OK" sign. His eyes were the color of unpolished emerald. I thought that strange—green eyes on an Asian. Hadn't thought of that before. His light drained from them and all that was left was the hint of his ancestors staring back, making gestures I could not interpret. They faded away in turn and left me with the prevernal calm of the ages. A cool breeze, like that of a teasing mistress, blew in my ear, across my neck, down my back, and I felt full. Slotted into a groove.

I had held his hand the entire time.

The entries that followed described more killings. A female VC LeGrange shot in the head in a village near Phuoc Thinh, three NVA cut down charging his foxhole near My Khe, an old man on the bank along the Thu Bon, his throat cut because LeGrange was curious if old skin would be more or less yielding. There were more than a dozen such entries. Sometimes LeGrange used his knife, sometimes his gun. One time, he killed a teen-aged boy hiding in an underground shelter with a grenade—white phosphorus, not anti-personnel—because he and Jo-Jo were curious to see what the burning phosphorus would do to a body.

Eventually LeGrange just recorded numbers.

4 April 1968: 3

16 April 1968: 2

Soon, even the dates disappeared.

It was now well past dusk. I had spent nearly two hours reading, horror-struck, and I was no closer to any kind of clarity or understanding. Not even a hint at what it was I was supposed to understand. That night, I tried to sleep, but much like one worries a painful tooth, I kept coming back to the nagging question of why. Why did LeGrange send this to me? My brother said he was just a crazy man who got fucked up in Vietnam, and the journals certainly seemed to confirm that. But was it that simple? Was this just another crazy act of a disturbed man? And if so, why send it to *me*? Why not Bryan? He seemed to know LeGrange; or at least, know of him. I didn't. What could LeGrange possibly have, then, to explain to *me*?

Despite a late-night resolution to destroy the journals in the morning and be rid of LeGrange once and for all, to solve the mystery by ignoring it, the next morning I made a pot of coffee and picked up the last journal:

LT's a problem. Baker overheard him talking to McKenna about us. Says we need to be reigned in. Told McKenna to keep an eye on us.

I'm not worried about Sarge. He's a soldier. I remember what he said one night back at base camp. "Some people don't want us here. Protest this war. Call it immoral, but, shit, I don't know anything about that one way or the other." He paused to pull on his beer. "I've been killing dinks for more than a decade now. Was killing them up in Korea for a spell, then they send me here to kill some more. Up there, down here, doesn't matter. Uncle Sam tells me to kill dinks, I kill dinks. I'll leave the right and the wrong of it to the politicians and the professors."

No, we won't have any problems with McKenna. He's a soldier. But we'll have to do something about LT.

That's all there seemed to be in the last journal. The rest, clean pages. But tucked behind the back cover were a handful of loose pages, torn out of the journal and then crammed back in. Unfolding theses pages, I read on.

Command told us to march to this ridge. Three days through what was once lush jungle before Mr. Orange got to play. Now we're here and LT "has doubts." Command says the village below this ridge is VC. We have orders to do a CA tomorrow, but that spineless fuck wants to do reconnaissance instead. "Reconnaissance," he calls it. "Pussy," is what I call it. LT is just a goddamned, born-yellow, pussy! We've marched for three days and now he's not going to let us have our fun? Fuck that! We've decided to do it ourselves.

These last pages were smeared in dirt and dried blood, an appropriate backdrop for the horrors the pages contained. Despite a screaming demand to close my eyes, to make the words go away, I pressed on. As I read those final pages, I grew faint. My legs rubbery, my mouth dusty and desiccated. I was no longer reading the journal of a person, a memoir of experience. What was before me on these pages was the death of a soul.

I wish they waited. It was so peaceful. The morning glories of the sky. The reds, the yellows, the oranges. And until they showed up, those glories were ours. Just the four of us.

"Look at that sky, brother," Jo-Jo said, gesturing at the sky with his knife.

I sat and appreciated it, unable to see it as anything other than a benediction.

"Almost as beautiful as napalm," I said.

Jo-Jo laughed and we exchanged our ritualized handshakes.

"My man. Cyrus the Virus. Once you busted your cherry, shit, you be like a force of nature. You enter the scene, people drop dead. You're a contagion, my man. A motherfucking contagion. Goddamn! I'm glad I'm no slope."

He then resumed working on his necklace, using the point of his knife to poke a hole in the oblong disc of flesh in his hand. Picking up a stretch of wire he cut from one of the pig corals, he snaked it through the hole and drew it through until the disc nestled against eight similar discs. Jo-Jo did a quick count, then asked me: "How many you think would be best? I got nine so far."

"How the fuck you get an odd number?"

"One of them got hit by Baker's little science project, one side of her head all fucked up."

I smiled, thinking of Baker's contraption. Two stolen mortar rounds wrapped together with wire, a WP grenade nestled between them like a keepsake.

"Yeah," I said. "That sure was pretty."

"Well, pretty or not, all it really did was wake up LT and the rest. They'll be here soon."

Jo-Jo shouted over his shoulder to Baker, "Thanks a lot, mother-fucker. 'Bout the last thing I want to see on this glorious morning is that goddamn cracker."

Baker was walking among the now-smoldering frames of what had been huts a few hours ago. His dick was in his hand, and he was pissing indiscriminately, spraying the frames and the ground around them, mumbling over and again, "Mine. Mine. Mine." He didn't answer Jo-Jo. Just grinned and gave us a friendly wave.

"What'd you think the LT will do?" I asked.

"Shit, that mother-fucker ain't gonna do a goddamned thing. He's gonna look at us like we just gangbanged his grandmother, and then he's gonna look away. War for him is chess and textbooks. He don't want any part of what this is. He's just gonna look away, gather himself, and then call it in to Command, report the village is secured. Now, how many do you think I need for this?" he asked again, holding up the necklace.

"I don't know. Twelve. Like donuts." I caught sight of Baker again. His back was slightly turned to us, so I could not be sure if he was still pissing on things or if he was now jerking-off.

"Thirteen," I said, inspired. "Make it a Baker's dozen."

Jo-Jo stood up, grinning. "I see what you did there, Virus." He walked over to an unharvested body, a woman, perhaps in her fifties, in black pajamas. He knelt over her and began to saw. A few moments later, he tilted her head and repeated the process.

"Eleven," he said, more to himself than to me, before he turned the corner of a hut none of us got around to firing yet.

I suspected we only had a handful of minutes before they got here. Five, maybe ten at most. I wanted to be with someone when they came. I didn't want to intrude on Baker's moment, so I went in search of Christianson.

I found him crouching in front of one of the village's firepits, slicing from a hunk of meat skewered over flame.

I sat down beside him; the expression on his face was distant, yet blissful. I'd seen this look before, at the Pentecostal revivals Momma took me to when I was young, on the men handling the snakes.

"Hey, Christianson." I felt embarrassed to break into the reverie. "What you eating?"

"Breakfast."

"Close enough to bacon, I reckon."

"It ain't pig."

"Didn't see a buffalo when we came in."

"Ain't buffalo, neither."

"I give up," I said with a chuckle, "what you eatin'?"

Christianson grinned, gristle and flecks of red spotting his teeth. "I already told you. Breakfast."

His held-up finger silenced any response. He cocked his head to the left, listening into the void. "LT's here," he said.

Christianson's announcement was the final line on the final page. I dropped the journal and loose pages and left them there, foolishly afraid of contagion. My brother was right. Just a crazy man who got fucked up in Vietnam. Nothing to do with me. But in the days and weeks that followed, I could not shake the feeling a shadow was dogging me. Lingering. Always just out of perception, but there. Haunting my dreams, stalking my days. Whispering with a dread certainty that LeGrange wasn't done with me yet.

3

On a Tuesday morning in April, Staff Sergeant Lance Charles drove to his V.A. appointment in Perry Point, Maryland. No one is quite sure what transpired between him and his doctor, Dr. Lynda Karl, because sometime during their scheduled appointment, Staff Sergeant Lance Charles strangled her with his belt. Dr. Karl's murder was not discovered until Staff Sergeant Charles had already left the building on his way home where he strangled Brandie, his lovely wife of six years—who had patiently played the role of Penelope during Staff Sergeant Charles's three successive deployments in Iraq—with the same belt he used on Dr. Karl. Based on ligature marks on her throat, investigators concluded Staff Sergeant Charles used his hands to strangle his beautiful baby girl, Melody, aged 5. Wanting to recognize his faithful friend, Max, as part of the family, Staff Sergeant Charles filled the golden retriever's food bowl with Old Roy mixed with a lethal dose of ground up cyclobenzaprine.

After sending his family on ahead (preceded, of course, by the good doctor), Staff Sergeant Charles put a Colt .45 ACP service pistol, the one his grandfather had carried at Guadalcanal, in his mouth and blew out the back side of his head.

Investigators later revealed that Staff Sergeant Charles had been seeing Dr. Karl three times a week since he returned from the desert, where he had narrowly-escaped death from an I.E.D. His three closest friends had not been as lucky. Staff Sergeant Charles reportedly had complained of difficulty sleeping, of confused, sometimes frightened, thoughts, and a sense of betrayal, of alienation and paranoia, steadily during the four months he had been home.

Like most others, I read the story of Staff Sergeant Lance Charles and was moved. Moved by the death of Dr. Karl, a *summa cum laude* graduate of Stanford University with an advanced degree from Columbia. She had a husband of seven years of mostly glorious marriage, who can now only sleep by aid of an increasingly-larger dose of pills. In the kind of odd coincidence that makes stories like these so disturbingly real, Dr. Karl also had a golden retriever named Max.

I was moved by the death of Brandie, who spent most of her time working as a volunteer at the local elementary school, her love of children bursting well beyond her instinctive call to keep Melody happy and safe. The children at Woodlawn Elementary miss her, write her letters and draw her pictures of families standing beneath yellow, circular, spoked suns and M-shaped birds.

I was moved by the death of little Melody. Aunts and uncles described her as precocious at loving and at generosity, but that may have been their grief talking. Her friends at school said she liked Krispy Kreme donuts (glazed), loved birds, and thought that a freckle-faced classmate, Tim Matthews, was cute. For his part, young Timmy Matthews just assumed they would grow up and get married, maybe "have a dozen kids."

I was moved by Timmy Matthews as well.

I was moved by Max. So blindly loyal, it could never occur to him that Staff Sergeant Charles, with whom he had taken so many walks, fetched so many balls, snuggled up on the couch so many days, could ever have anything but his best interests at heart. Max had instinctively felt there was something wrong with Staff Sergeant Charles, that he was damaged in some way, but obviously was unable to convey this knowledge. So, Max just loved him more, snuggled him closer.

I was moved by the other Max as well, who will spend countless afternoons by the kitchen door, waiting in vain for Dr. Karl to come home.

But what surprised me most about the sad, tragic story of Staff Sergeant Lance Charles, is that I found myself moved by PFC Cyrus LeGrange. Many of the later stories about Staff Sergeant Charles featured recollections by friends, family, and neighbors about comments Staff Sergeant Charles had said, about odd but now understandable behaviors of his, all now identified as "a cry for help."

Was this what LeGrange's journals were? Was what he sent me a cry for help? Was his post-war trauma driving him toward a similar catastrophic finish?

After reading for days successive stories about Staff Sergeant Lance Charles, I recalled those pages that had slipped out of the last journal, the ones about the village, about Jo-Jo's necklace of ears, of Christianson's unspeakable meal. On the back of one of those pages, written in the palsied scrawl of the postcards, I read:

The things I've done will circle back. A death foretold is but a death delayed. I hope that the end, if nothing else, will be glorious.

These words haunted me now. Was LeGrange planning to go out like Staff Sergeant Charles? Was that what he meant by a glorious end? And if so, if the journals were indeed a cry for help, no matter how oddly addressed—for I was still at a loss why they were sent to me—did I not have a responsibility here? If not to LeGrange, then what about to those others who would be caught up in the debris field of his glorious ending? Would they not be collateral damage, that term so favored by the military to describe incidental innocents? And could I live with that?

4

Hico was just like any of the other central Texas small towns I drove through to get there. The suggestion of rolling hills, strands of scrub oak, small local stores lining a town square at the center of which stood a needlessly elaborate town hall; weeds here were renamed mesquite trees, giving the illusion of intention to what was merely loss of control.

LeGrange lived two miles outside of town. A long dirt driveway snaked from the road past a small pond to a white stuccoed house surrounded by crepe myrtles of red and purple. There was a one-level brick and stone house horizoned on a small ridge about two hundred yards away.

The door only opened a few inches in response to the doorbell.

"Yes?" The voice behind the blue eye peeking out was gravelly and shaky, the vocal equivalent of the handwriting on the postcards.

"Mr. LeGrange?"

The cracked door narrowed. "Who wants to know?"

"I'm Michael."

My name the magic word. The door a sideways gap-toothed smile, and there he stood—Cyrus LeGrange.

The left side of his body sagged, like a string that was holding it up had been cut. His face was long, like a candle that had been melted and allowed to cool again, topped with graying, flat-topped stubble. Cracked lips moved in an attempted smile and LeGrange extended his hand in greeting. When I took it, he pulled, jerking me off my feet into his unexpected embrace.

"I wouldn't have never thought this," he cried.

I was swallowed up by Texas hospitality, given a rocking chair on the porch and a cold, sweating glass of sweet tea.

"Your brother used to come over and we'd fish in that pond," LeGrange said. "Near about every evening for a while. He'd catch a sunny and I'd unhook it, throw it back, and in a little while, he'd catch another sunny. He was always convinced it was the same fish. Asked it 'why don't you learn?'" LeGrange chuckled at the memory.

"And that garden out back, your father helped me put that in. And whenever Carol and I had to go somewhere, take a little trip or to stay overnight at the V.A. your father took care of it for me." He paused and then faltered, "Your father . . . your father was a good man."

We ate a meal of chili con carne and cornbread, and then were back out on the porch, with home-made whiskey standing in for the afternoon's sweet tea. His wife joined us for about an hour before she excused herself, admonishing us to "not stay up too late." LeGrange refilled our glasses one more time and I wanted to ask all of the accumulated whys, but found to my surprise I could not do so with ease. LeGrange radiated a peace, seemed soothed, healed. Breaking into that seemed abominably rude. Like picking the scab off someone else's wound.

"I read the journals," I said finally, looking into the dark Texas night instead of him.

After a silence that made me question whether he heard, he said, "I appreciate that."

"What happened to Jo-Jo and the rest?"

"Jo-Jo got himself killed in Detroit. Broke into an old lady's house. Shot her. Barricaded himself in her house for three days before the cops flushed him out. Baker got himself committed a few years after we got back. He died in a mental hospital, up near where he grew up, oh, I reckon about fifteen, twenty years ago. Don't know what happened to Christianson. He ran off the night before we were sent home. Said he was staying. Just walked off into the jungle, and the jungle closed right up after him."

This last said in a barely-audible whisper.

"I was a bright boy before they sent me out. Was headed for college. Thought I might like to be a professor of something. History, maybe. Or maybe a writer. Used to be able to write something strong. But that place," he gestured wildly with his right hand, "took all that. Left something else in its place. Not sure what."

He turned and looked me in the eye, saw the line of questions I had waiting behind mine, and said,

"Not yet. Not tonight."

He knocked back the rest of his drink and stood up.

"Carol made up the guest room for you. Down the hall, first door on the right. I expect you'll be comfortable." Then he turned and disappeared into the darkness of the house.

There was a cold pressure on my check, waking me from a fitful and image-haunted sleep. Flashes of moonlight danced along the serrated blade of a knife and beyond that, LeGrange's flat, gleaming eyes.

"I wanted you'd be better" he hissed. "Not a piss-poor assassin."

He spat out the last word like a piece of rancid flesh, and pressed the knife point harder. I felt blood trickle down my cheek like a tear. The skin around his nose pinched in preparation for a final thrust. I held my last breath and waited, looking into his eyes as he searched through mine, past my fear into the something beyond. What he saw there left him unsteady, confused.

"She never told you."

"Who? Told me what?"

"Your mother. I wouldn't have never thought that."

"Never told me what?"

LeGrange didn't answer. Just took a bandana from his back pocket, tossed it to me, and walked out of the room.

I found him out on the front porch, rocking in his chair. He was muttering or chanting something so low under his breath that I had to lean in close in order to make it out:

"They let out the genie. They shouldn't have done that."

Just that. Over and over again. "They let out the genie. They shouldn't have done that."

"Mr. LeGrange?"

LeGrange looked up. "Once you do, you can't get it back in."

"Get *what* back in?"

"The genie."

"What genie."

"Me. I'm the genie."

A shudder rippled through his body and when it passed, I was staring at the more lucid LeGrange of this afternoon's sweet tea.

"When we first got to Vietnam," he said as I settled into the chair beside him, "we were all afraid of dying. Then we became afraid we'd run out of slants to kill. That's what they did to us. We were just boys. Then we turned into something else. They say that was war, as if that excuses it."

I didn't know what to say, so I stayed silent.

"I'll never forget the air over there. I remember being so surprised it could hold so much sound. It was so humid, so over-saturated, that I didn't think there'd be room."

Somewhere in the dark, an owl screeched. Frogs chirruped. Coyotes yipped to each other across a void.

"The air was like that on the day you were born," LeGrange continued. "So humid even the water was getting wet." He chuckled softly before continuing. "The plan, the plan your parents worked out with us when it was clear it was about your time, was that her parents would drive down from North Dakota when they got the call. It would take them the best part of two days to get down here. In the meantime, they'd call cousins of your mother who lived in Tulsa. It would take them about eight hours to get down here. In the meantime, one of your father's work friends was to drive over to your place, stay with Bryan until the cousins got here. And I was to stay with Bryan until the friend got here.

"That was the plan. But I didn't think much about that when I heard pounding on my door at three in the morning. In fact, I don't remember thinking anything, one way or the other. A moment just presented itself. Jury said I must have thought someone was breaking in. I don't know anything about that. But what I do know, is that on the day you were born, I blew your daddy near in half with my shotgun. Gave him both barrels. Cops say I reloaded and gave him both barrels again, dead as he was, but I don't know nothing about that neither. All I know is that I killed your daddy. I'm sorry I did it. And I hope whatever it is that brought you here, brought you here to forgive."

Somewhere in the dark, an owl screeched. Frogs chirruped. Coyotes yipped to each other across a void.

He wanted forgiveness, and I left Texas letting him think he had it. I'm not sure why I did that. Maybe I felt he had suffered enough. Maybe I felt it wasn't for me to forgive. After all, in a sense he was more my father, with his postcards, his keeping track of me, than the two-dimensional image I saw in pictures in family albums. If I never knew my father, how could I weigh the lack, how could I know what there was to forgive? There was a man, who was supposed to be in my life, who wasn't. There are lots of things that are *supposed* to be in our lives that aren't. How do you weigh them against each other? How do you assign value? How do you claim grievance or ask forgiveness?

5

I was in D.C., freelancing a story, when I learned of LeGrange's death. His wife wrote to me about it. Said she knew I'd want to know? How did she know that? As with everything else about LeGrange, questions begat further questions, not answers.

LeGrange was riding his bike along one of the country roads outside Hico when an old, battered pick-up truck with two locals "with outspoken racial views" (so said the press clipping Carol included with her letter) ran him off the road. They then circled back after one of them (according to witnesses) had climbed into the truck bed, where he took down a rifle from the gun rack on the back of the cab, took careful aim, and shot Cyrus LeGrange.

The article speculated as to motivation. Perhaps they mistook LeGrange for an Hispanic. Or perhaps they misinterpreted his dark, Mediterranean coloration as an indication of Jewishness, and thus it was their Anti-Semitism, and not their more generalized racism, that got LeGrange killed.

I crumpled up the article and tossed it into a nearby trash can. What did it matter, their motivation? Why this continual drive to ask for reasons? To assign blame? Someone let out a genie and couldn't get it back in. And as a result, a moment presented itself. Simple as that.

Later that afternoon, I took a cab to the National Mall and made my way over to the long black granite walls. More than 58,000 names were inscribed on these walls, but not Cyrus LeGrange's. I traced my way past the "K's" and found where it would have been. Right there, between SSG William Francis LeGrand and 1LT Arthur Russell LeGrow, Jr.

I then made my way towards the front of the wall, toward the "B's" and found the narrow space between the names of PO3 Stephen Cornell Brunton and SGT Robert Michael Brupbacher. The space that should read Michael James Bruntson. Wasn't he, just as much as Cyrus

LeGrange, a casualty of war? And what did that make me, bearer of the same name?

Above me, the sun had set behind a bank of clouds, illuminating them, red and purple. They looked like a raw wound, the scab picked off.

Hadron

"For the want of a nail the shoe was lost."

1

Years from now, long after the divorce, Louis would recognize all the signs he had missed. The clarions screaming that Molly was, to put it mildly, not as invested in the relationship as he was. Her refusal to take his name ("'Draper' sounds too much like 'rape her.'"). The quickly-closed windows that seemed to be Tinder ("damn pop-up ads"). Her insistence that when she was away at conventions, *she* would call *him* ('it just makes more sense, logistically. You know how conventions are; tightly-packed schedules with a layer of unpredictable chaos on top.").

But the crystal clarity of her "serial infidelity"—as he would term it in the post-divorce years when people asked—was far in the future. Today was about the phone call. The one Louis made—in bold and direct contradiction of Molly's rule—when she was in Vegas this past weekend. The phone call a man answered.

They left the kids at home and walked to the park just off Classen and 36th, sat on a bench and talked, Molly's face wearing a mask of stylized contrition, Louis's one of constrained placidity, one meant to suggest there was nothing to see here, that everything was fine. For above all things, even the heart-piercing stab of cuckoldry, Louis feared embarrassment most. In his mind, a humiliation was only a humiliation if it was noticed by others.

Once they were seated, Molly—reading her cue, ever the performer—reached over and took Louis's hand in hers.

"I'm so sorry," she said.

"Who was he?"

"Just a guy."

"I gathered that from the phone call. Care to narrow it down a bit?"

"Just a guy at a convention. Living it up, you know? What happens in Vegas."

"Except this didn't stay in Vegas, did it?" Louis tried to barb.

Like an ophthalmologist switching lenses, Molly replaced contrition with a modest, embarrassed, but slightly hopeful smile.

"No, it didn't. And if I could take it back, I would."

Because the divorce was still in the future, Louis did not realize the "it" meant different things to each of them.

"Great, he's an educator too. So, you'll run into him at other conventions, I assume."

"No, he was there for a different convention. He's a scientist."

"Oh, how exciting. I hope he wore his pocket protector."

Molly allowed him the caustic joke. He certainly was entitled to that, at the very least. Although the thrust of the comment hit a little too close to home, made her think of the broken condom, how blithely-dismissive, alcohol-lubricated as they were, both she and Hans had been about it. But Molly was nothing if not careful. Careful and calculating. She made sure Louis made love to her the night she returned. Just in case worst came to worst. And she did things that night she didn't normally do. With Louis, at least. Banking on the hope that there was nothing more mollifying than Paternity-Masking Sex.

And it did the trick. Louis never knew. Or if he did, he kept it to himself. Because a humiliation was only a humiliation if it was noticed by others.

But all that was in the future, In the now, she just squeezed Louis's hand harder, hoping he'd find it a comfortable reaffirmation of something never actually affirmed in the first place.

"It was really just a random thing, honey. And it will *never* happen again. I promise. Plus, he doesn't even live here. He's French. Lives in Switzerland."

As if distance and place mattered.

2

Carter Hicks hated himself. A deep-seated, latent hatred that came out every other day. How else to explain why he would subject himself to jogging through the searing petri dish of an Oklahoma summer?

And to make matters worse, his normal stopping point—a specific spot that became his sole mental focus during the last two hundred yards of his 2.5-mile run, each step grudgingly tractor-beamed by this fantasized stopping point—was not available. Seated on his normal bench, a couple were engaged in a fight masked as normal conversation.

Carter had to recalibrate on the fly, refocus his energies onto the next bench, some four dozen extra, excruciating steps further down the path. The modern marathon is 26.2 miles. The extra distance was added in 1908, during the Olympic games in London. Queen Alexandra wanted the Royal Box to be the finish line. Carter had been told by his few marathon friends that during that last, arbitrarily-added leg of a marathon, it is typical to curse that royal bitch.

For the first time, Carter's understanding of this anger was not academic. Carter may have hated himself, but in each of those extra, unnecessary, agonizing steps, he hated that couple more.

As he staggered into and then onto the new benchmark, he wanted to shoot the fighting couple a glare laced with all the accumulated malice of each extra step. But he was too worn out to do so. He was too worn out to do a lot of things, like notice the crumpled up brown paper bag he landed on when he collapsed onto the bench. For what seemed hours (for such is the randomness of experiential time) he was too worn out to do anything other than sweat a sweat more akin to melting.

Eventually, Carter returned to himself, could breathe deeply every fourth breath, then every third, then normally again. And that's when he finally noticed the bag.

He heard it before he saw it. The rattling of small objects from inside the bag called out to him with the atavistic pull of a longed-for noise from our collective childhoods. So much so that Carter rattled the bag some more before he looked inside and gazed upon such an incongruous gathering of randomness. A description of the contents of the bag requiring such an odd pairing of words that Carter found himself muttering them between pulls of Gatorade and disbelief:

"Drugs, blood, and a Playbill."

Over and again, Carter mumbled, "Drugs, blood, and a Playbill."

3

"You gotta call the police," Violet said, her voice laden with a panic the phone line did little to smother.

"Don't you think that's a bit over-reactive?" Carter asked.

"Carter, I'm serious. *This* is serious. Don't fuck around. Call the police."

Because he was stung by the implication of her "*This* is serious," how it whispered that he wasn't, he wanted to sting back.

"I didn't call you for legal advice."

He seemed to land his shot, his insecurity touching on her own, for the panic now left her voice, replaced by cold, grainy distance.

"Why *did* you call?"

If Carter did not appreciate the implication of her comment before, he liked the implication of that distance even less. He recognized it. All too well. In all the years he had known Violet, from Mrs. Grace's kindergarten, all through junior then senior high school, his haphazard attempts to follow her to community college, the failed attempt to follow her down to Norman, through all of that, Carter learned to recognize that voice, the unbridgeable distance ladled into it.

The distance was her self-retreat, a pull back to an internal nugget of self she let no one else near. Like a turtle within its shell, Violet would pull herself inside, and shut off whoever was around. Carter had heard this voice over the years when Violet readied herself to end relationships, with her parents, with stagnant high school friends, and, of most personal interest to Carter, with her now ex-boyfriends. His greatest fear through all these years was that he'd hear the voice directed at him, that he would one day find himself shut off.

"I just meant you were pre-med, not pre-law," he joked, praying for mollification.

And because she also feared shutting Carter off (although he did not know this), she accepted, gratefully, the gift.

"OK. Fair enough. But I'm serious about going to the cops. That sounds like a lot of drugs."

"Yeah, that was one of the questions I had for you. So, there's no way that's just someone's prescription I found?"

"Carter, no doctor is going to prescribe *both* Vicodin and Oxy. And no doctor is going to prescribe that much of either. You said you had over two hundred pills of each?"

"Yeah. What wasn't in the prescript bottles were sealed in packs of four."

"Yeah, that is *so* drug-dealing stuff. You don't want any part of this."

Again, the suggestion that Carter couldn't handle something serious, but he let this one go. Because he knew that she was probably right.

"The other question I have was about the blood. It seemed a lot."

"It always does."

"But how much is too much? What if this Alex guy is dead?"

"You would need to lose much more than what you described. And, I can't believe the guy's name was on the prescription bottles. That doesn't seem very smooth-criminal."

"Oh, it wasn't. It was on the Playbill. An inscription inside."

"Oh, right, the Playbill. That's what makes this weird instead of just scary. What play was it?"

"*The Iceman Cometh.*"

There was a silence on the line, which Carter tried to jokingly fill.

"Oh, don't tell me you're an English major now, in addition to your pre-law expertise."

It was a gamble, pushing once again at the door he knew she wouldn't open, but he got away with it, because it wasn't the play that had Violet silent, it was some other piece of information he offered, a different puzzle piece slotting into place.

"Anything thing else you want to ask?" she said.

There *was* something else Carter wanted to ask, something he had wanted to ask since the first time they were paired up in gym class, square dancing in first grade, but he wouldn't ask it now. The inertia of habit is a hard thing to break free of.

"Please, Carter," Violet said one more time before getting off the phone, "Go to the police. Turn over the bag and let them deal with it. Please." Her voice once again laden with a panic the phone line did little to smother.

4

"God made us so that as we get older, we get more disgusted with the world, so that when we die, it's not that big a deal. That is the shape and the form of His mercy."

Auguste Cameratto took a long, cold sip of iced tea from the sweating glass, swirled it savoringly with a relish that seemed to belie his statement. "I've now reached the point where the best argument I have against death is that I'll miss having an iced tea on a scorching hot Oklahoma summer day."

He looked off towards where the sunset would eventually be, and said, as if forgetting he was having a conversation, "and that's not really enough to miss."

Natrillo had to agree, at least with the scorching hot part. Despite living in Oklahoma since a young boy, he had never fully gotten used to the summer heat.

"Yeah," he said. "We should've listened to that Al Gore guy, I suppose."

"It wouldn't have mattered. Most people have no real commitment to their own best interests. Which is, of course, the foundation of crime. So, I'm not complaining." He took another savoringly slow sip of iced tea, before shrugging at Natrillo and adding, "I'd rather rule in Hell, as they say."

Natrillo didn't know how to reply. No matter how often he came here, he was thrown off-balance. One would be hard pressed to imagine a less-likely setting for a mob boss like Cameratto. Greenland, maybe? A rainforest, somewhere? But Oklahoma would have to be on the short list.

Of course, he'd been told the stories, the history, since he was a child. He understood the rationale behind it. How the *Cosa Nostra* had been using the town of Krebs as a favorite hideaway, a place to lay low until a heat dies down (the thought made Natrillo chuckle. The very idea of heat dying down in this land of unrelenting summer sun seemed surreal if not ridiculous).

And then there was Cameratto himself. A one-time member of The Commission. A legend. For much of Natrillo's youth, a boogeyman his mother threatened him with. "Behave," she'd said, waving a wooden spoon in his direction, "or I'll send you over to *Signore* Cameratto, let him deal with you" before returning to the stove and her ambrosial red sauce.

Cameratto had been sent to Krebs nearly thirty years ago, after a dust-up with the Gambino family in which some feelings—and things more permanent than feelings—had been hurt. He'd been sent out here to remove a target of convenience. Of course, the Gambinos could have gotten to him out here, called Ambrose or one of the others, but the idea of moving him was like that of having one of those steering wheel locks in your car. Sure, a car thief could still drive your car away if they wanted to, but the moderate inconvenience of the lock usually made other, non-locked cars more appealing.

And it worked. They were content to whack Carmine Lucressi. Felt that made their point well enough. And either no one thought to call Cameratto back, or he simply decided to stay. Although, as to the latter possibility, Natrillo, his Brunello Cucinelli soaked through as if he had just emerged from a swim in the pond with the fountain inside the development's main gate, sometimes struggled to see how anyone would *choose* to stay. Maybe what

Cameratto just said—that he'd "rather rule in Hell"—explained it as well as anything.

More disconcerting than Cameratto choosing to stay in Oklahoma was Cameratto himself. Once anointed a future *capo*, now nothing but desiccated husk. Not geriatric, but over-weathered, like an old baseball glove left out in too many thunderstorms to dry under too many suns. If it wasn't for the memorized iconography, the rings of sapphire and opal, the St. Christopher medallion, the gold chain with an obsidian cross, Natrillo would hardly believe this was the same man his mother once threatened him with.

Most disconcerting to Natrillo, when he allowed himself to think on it, was the fact that years after these boogeyman threats he found himself working for Cameratto. Such serendipity could be, if one spent too much time pondering it, terrifying.

"*Signore* Cameratto," he began into the silence.

"Please," Cameratto interrupted, "Auguste. We've known each other far too long to stand on such formalities."

"Auguste, we have a bit of a situation."

"You think I don't know about it?" Cammeratto asked, a slight chuckle lacing his cracked voice, the spider well aware of what goes on in every corner of its web.

"Well, I've got good news and bad news."

"You found Alex?"

"No. That's the bad news. Still no sign of him."

"So we have no idea if he's alive or dead?"

"No idea."

"And the good news?"

Natrillo held up the brown paper sack, jiggled it like a rattle.

"You couldn't have put them in something else?"

"Evidence bags are counted."

Cameratto waved away the topic. "So, we have the drugs back but no word on our distributor?"

"That looks about the size of it. And it's just dumb luck we got the drugs. Some kid was jogging in Memorial Park, found the bag, called it in."

"Good Samaritan."

"Yeah, well, even there we got lucky. He talked to Pendergast when he first called. Set up a time to come in. But then Pendergast called in sick this morning. Stomach bug. Some bad sushi. Anyway, he doesn't eat that bad sushi, the kid gives this bag to him instead of me. See what I mean? You got lucky."

"I pay you to *be* my luck," Cameratto said in a voice not meant to be as chilling as it was.

"So, my question for you, Danny Boy," he continued, "is who took a shot, or several shots, at Alex? Is this about Alex? Or is this about the drugs? In short, Officer Natrillo, is someone trying to muscle in on my action?"

"I don't know. Yet. Maybe the McDonald brothers?"

Cameratto did not respond immediately. He looked back off to the horizon, pulled another mouthful of iced tea, and began to mumble in a low, singsong voice:

"Old McDonald had a farm. E-I-E-I-O. And on this farm, he cooked some meth. E-I-E-I-O."

Natrillo stiffened, unsure if this was dementia or horror speaking. But then Cameratto returned, locked eyes with Natrillo once again.

"I don't think so. Our understanding has, I believe, been mutually-beneficial. Chase is too smart, I think, to mess with that." Cameratto then sighed. "But the younger brother? He's untethered. Too excitable for this business." He sighed again before concluding, "I'll look into it. What about the Good Samaritan? Any chance he's in play?"

"He doesn't look the part."

"None of us look the part. Keep an eye on him."

"Will do. And the McDonald brothers? You want me to keep an eye on them too?"

"No. Like I said, I'll look into it."

5

"There's someone in Oklahoma named Giuseppe?"

"Five million people in this state. I imagine there's two or three."

"And you hired him?"

"Yup."

"To do what?"

"To be our driver."

"Without asking me?"

"You weren't around."

"So, you brought a guy into our business based on one Uber ride? And you think that somehow makes some kinda sense? How do you know he's not a narc? And that him picking you up wasn't a set up?"

"Because he wasn't supposed to be my ride. I had a scheduled pick up through Lyft, which is usually cheaper than Uber. But by the time I landed, got my bags, and got outside, my Lyft driver had been and gone. So, I checked Uber, and just like that, G was there, ready and willing."

"G?"

"Yeah. He prefers to be called G."

"Of course he does."

"So, relax, Little Brother. There's no way this was a set up."

"Why we need a driver anyway," Rye asked

"Until meth learns to fly or walk on its own," Chase replied, "it needs to get from Point A to Point B somehow. And what better cover than an Uber driver? Cops don't hassle Uber drivers."

"And why's that?"

"Because they keep DUIs down. Let cops focus on the more enjoyable aspects of their job, like shooting minorities and torquing favors from the whores. So, no random stops of Uber drivers. And if an Uber rolls a Stop sign, no worries. If an Uber runs an orange light, no worries. And if an Uber . . . "

"Is hauling our meth," Rye finished for him, "no worries."

"Now you're getting it," Chase said.

"But why him?"

"Wait until you see him drive. At first, that constant tweaking with his eyes? Looking all around, in the mirrors and everything? Shit, I thought he was one of our customers. But he's always analyzing, always anticipating. Looking at all the angles, predicting where the next complication could come from? Where will the trouble be? Who's the shitty driver? Who didn't see the merge lane? Who's in a hurry, liable to be reckless? I'm telling you, other people are driving cars, he's playing chess. Little Brother, finding this guy was pure serendipity. That means 'lucky.'"

Rye hated when his brother used big words like that. He hated it even more when his brother defined them condescendingly to him. He finished the last bite of BBQ, waded up his napkin, and arched it at the trashcan in the corner. It bounced off the rim, onto the floor. He added the pique of the witnessed missed shot to that of his brother's condescension.

"Lyft is cheaper," Rye teased, playfully punching his brother in the shoulder, harder than a tease should allow—he made that concession to his annoyance—but not hard enough to escalate anything. "You fucking cheapskate," he added.

"Little Brother, we are running a business. And a business is a business."

Chase knew his brother well enough to know he was approaching a yellow. It didn't take much. And it didn't take much more to push into red.

"Hey," he said, mollifying, "let's head over to Fancy's; get some lunch; see the tittie-women. What'da say? A little burger and boob?"

And since they were running a business, and a business is a business, he added, "How did it go with Alex? You work things out?"

6

Rye had to admit his brother was right. That's what it was like. Watching someone play chess. But Rye also had to admit he didn't like it, this new wrinkle to the operation. Not one bit. Nor did he like this driver. Giuseppe?!? What the fuck kinda name was Giuseppe? What did he think this was, *Pinocchio?* (Rye winced, recalling his brother's mocking laughter when he asked this. He didn't understand what was so funny and he didn't like being laughed at. In fact, his brother was about the only person he'd let get away with that. But even then, there were limits to what he was willing to put up with).

There were a lot of things Rye didn't like. He didn't like the name his parents gave him. Ryan is a character in a soap opera. Ryan is not a tough guy. And Rye was most certainly that. So he shortened it, added the "e,"—"you know," he'd tell people worth telling, "like the whiskey."

He didn't like his parents. But that was no longer an issue.

And he didn't like his brother making decisions without him. Like hiring this driver.

And he didn't like *him*. No, there was no way around it. For starters, he was silent. In the way a mountain is silent. Or an ocean. It was disconcerting. Preternatural. Dude made him think of Michael Myers, or Jason, from those old horror flicks. Inexorable. *That* was the word for it. (Rye winced again, recognizing that the only reason he had access to such words was because he hears Chase use them). This guy was inexorable. Like a glacier.

And his eyes. There was something about the guy's eyes when he drove (or maybe all the time, who knew?). He got like in a trance when he drove. And his eyes. Like watching Shark Week. The eyes of a great white taking a bite. Empty, lifeless eyes. Like he didn't have a care in the world. Rye always thought that phrase meant something good. A status to be envied, to aspire towards. Until he got in the back seat of the car and watched "G" (as Chase insisted on calling him) drive, and saw there was a horror lurking within that phrase.

And getting him to talk? To say something? Fuck! That was like taking a shit that wasn't ready. And when you did get him to say something, you didn't know what the hell he was saying.

"Giuseppe, huh?" Rye prodded, and got nothing.

"What's your last name?" He prodded again, and again got nothing.

"You're driving a Prius (and of course he drove a fucking Prius!) at 55 miles-per-hour on the highway, so your last name sure as fuck ain't Andretti."

Nothing. Unless a cautious lane change counted as a response.

"You don't drive stick?" Rye tried one last time. "I thought all getaway drivers drive stick."

"I'm not a getaway driver. Getaway drivers are too narrow, focus on the wrong thing."

"And what's that?"

"Getting away."

Rye gave an incredulous chuckle. "Oh yeah? And what is it *you* focus on?"

"On driving."

7

When Violet told Carter he didn't want any part of this, it was only because she had a real clear idea what "this" was. She was smart enough to know where she was stupid, and where she was consistently stupid was her choice in boyfriends. She had a regrettable list of ex's. First there was Alex, who specialized in prescripts and acting, then there was Chase, the chem major she met during her run through the pre-med requirements and with whom she stayed for a while after he elected to pursue a more lucrative—if decidedly less legal—use of his chemical knowledge.

She sighed as she massaged her elbow, still sore from being wrenched behind her, and thought of Carter. He was not on that list of ex's. They'd been bouncing around each other since they were little kids, but there was never the collision. She wondered—not for the first time—what her life would've been like if there had been. Or would be. She often joked that her name was one letter shy of "violent," and she had to admit, with just a small, sad hint of despair, that that summed up her life quite well. She seemed to be always connected at one remove from violence.

Because that was the thing about her list of ex's. When you dated a drug dealer, you didn't just date the drug dealer. You dated the world of drug dealing. A world of message-sending, of territory feuds, of a baseline of codified aggression.

You dated their whole world. Which sometimes included a younger brother, too excitable for such a business. A younger brother who a short while ago forced his way into her apartment, who wrenched her arm behind her, twisted, demanded to know where the ex that preceded his brother would lie low, who told her he needed to go finish the job, needed to take care of the loose ends.

She flexed her arm back and forth, rubbing the elbow, working the pain slowly away. She understood how this would play out. Rye wouldn't stop at Alex; his rage, once kindled, was a whirlwind. The cartoon Tasmanian Devil. Carter definitely did not want any part of this. But regardless, as one of those loose ends Rye braggartly threatened to take care of, it was just a matter of time, she feared, until he was most certainly a part of it.

8

Cameratto sat within the dim of Roma's sepia light, slowly chewing a mouthful of fresh bread, still warm from the oven, the busboy had just delivered. Auguste didn't recognize him. Must be new, hired since his last visit. He had the condensed litheness of a runner, the furrowed brow of someone piecing out a puzzle. Puzzle couldn't be job related, Auguste mused, savoringly sipping red wine. Being a busboy is fairly straightforward. Must be life weighing him down.

Auguste made a mental note to ask the kid about it. For all the media presentation of mob bosses, the unrestrained excesses, the hair-trigger violence—and not that Auguste didn't know too many colleagues who fit that description—he had always felt that *Signore* status came with a responsibility for benevolence. The point of being in a position of power was to use that position to help as many people as you could. At least that's how he saw it. That was a significant factor in his long-ago decision to stay in Krebs once the heat from the Gambinos simmered down.

He stayed. And he helped. Many people. People like the McDonald brothers. He gave them protection, allowed them to consolidate almost all of the meth trade in OKC, in exchange for tribute, and for keeping an eye on his many business ventures in the city. Ventures that included illegal 'scripts. It was a relationship of mutual benefit for these last few years.

But then that little shit Rye apparently felt he wanted in on the 'scripts. Or so it appeared. Cameratto took another long sip, held it, swished it around his teeth before swallowing, half lost in contemplation of the just-concluded conversation with Chase.

"*Signore* Cameratto . . ."

"Please. Auguste."

"Auguste. I know how it looks. Your dealer gets attacked; your drugs go missing."

"Alex was steady. Reliable. Like you used to be."

"I still am. You can still rely on me." There was desperation in Chase's voice, but, Auguste considered, he would be more concerned if there wasn't.

"But your brother," he began.

"It was personal."

"Excuse me?"

"The thing between Rye and Alex. It wasn't business. It was personal."

Cameratto bore into Chase, sizing him up, looking for tells, and came away satisfied.

"I'm glad about that. That suggests we can continue."

Across the table, the stress visibly slid away. Chase did not so much relax as he deflated.

"Thank you, *Signore* Cameratto."

Auguste held up a cautionary hand. "But your brother, whatever his motives, has created a mess. Sure, the drugs have been returned, but my inside guy tells me some glory-hound heading the drug task force in the OKCPD caught the faintest whiff of the story, and is now starting to look at things he didn't know to look at before. Added to that, I hear your brother went and finished the job with Alex."

"He was tying up loose ends."

"Well, whatever you want to call it, now there's a dead body, which means more cops looking at things they wouldn't be looking at if not for your brother."

Chase did not respond because there was no response.

"So," Cameratto concluded, steepling his hands and leaning on the table, "what, exactly, are we going to do about it?"

Now, his just delivered meal of shrimp scampi steaming before him, Cameratto reflected on the new agreement. The McDonalds would add 50% to this month's payment, for the inconvenience this dust-up had caused. And they would cover this month's payment to Natrillo, for he would be essential eyes and ears for them all until this blew over.

For the most part, he was satisfied. He believed Chase. This wasn't an attempt at muscling in on Cameratto's territory. Mostly because such an attempt would be quite unwise, and Chase—no matter what his brother was—was not dumb. But there was something that lingered, something that nagged, as he set to his lunch. What was that phase Chase used? About Rye "tying up loose ends." Yeah, that's what was nagging at him. He too needed to tie up loose ends. Cameratto coughed, trying to dislodge a haphazardly-chewed shrimp from his throat. For something this simple (for Cameratto foresaw no serious complications), it was probably not cost-effective to call in one of the big dogs. No need for Big Tuna or Ambrose, he reflected as he coughed again. Pollard, he decided, would do. Still expensive, but Cameratto was long of the mind that expense should never be the primary concern; using the exact right tool for a job should be. And, in this case, Pollard was most certainly the right tool for this job.

Cameratto would have thought some more about this, but the shrimp lodged in his throat demanded more of his attention, then his lungs demanded more oxygen, and then the floor demanded he show a basic obeisance to the laws of gravity.

9

He was a node, an intersection, the overlap of the Venn diagram, the metronome. And in a world ruled by chaos, it is the metronome that calls the tune. He was steady, patient, and calm. There were patterns in the chaos. Always. And the secret to his success lay in his ability to sniff them out. One can make predictions within the chaos if one simply pays attention. That's all it took.

That is why he drove. Why he filled the time when his boss did not need him with Uber rides. Driving was the only time he felt fully calm, moving within the patterns, making his way through the chaos. People didn't just have body language within themselves; they transferred it to their cars. The impatient wobble presaged a driver in a hurry, a driver who in a few seconds will cut you off. The driver looking down at their phone will not notice they're in an exit lane until after the last second, will panic and swerve into yours. You avoided these problems by making allowances for them before they happen.

Being a driver had nothing to do with speed and very little to do with the road. It had everything to do with patterns and predictions.

That's one of the things the excitable, tow-headed meth dealer didn't get. He just wanted Giuseppe to drive fast. Didn't understand the Prius, how it was vital to any successful "getaway." A getaway wasn't about getting away, but about moving through patterns, adopting them, using them to sustain movement, and allowing them to let those interested in preventing a getaway to fool themselves.

The best drivers didn't drive fast; they drove steady, as if their presence on that road was the most common, the most unnoteworthy thing there could be. Giuseppe could no longer count the number of times he was driving and placidly watched the "chasing" cop cars drive right past him as he muddled along in the center lane, holding steady at the posted speed limit, while the hardened criminals he was driving bitched and whined and panicked in the back seat. Didn't understand it was always the car jerking and screeching away from the scene that gets noticed. That set the chase in motion. A description of a car made invisible by commonplace is never made because it is never noticed.

Giuseppe tried to explain this to the excitable kid as he drove him to see the granddaughter, but the kid wasn't interested. They seldom were. No, the kid just wanted to flex his muscle, rough up on someone he thought weaker (if he only knew), and soon returned, the shallow pride of insignificant action beaming across his features, a little man reaffirming how big he thought he was.

He came out with an address, a second stop, which meant Giuseppe would be late. This caused him a little concern as he sat outside the second location, waiting for the kid to "finish that fuck," (for the kid also talked too much; the rule of "steady, patient and calm" had a verbal relevance as well) by which, Giuseppe mused, he meant a killing. Poor Alex, he thought. Giuseppe had driven him a few times to the theater, for auditions, rehearsals. He liked Alex. To the modest extent that he pulled for people (for it was patterns primarily that Giuseppe liked, not people), he pulled for him. Thought one day he'd catch a matinee, see Alex on stage; a few times when he was oozing through traffic he wondered if Alex might make it out. Now he knew.

As if on cue, the kid burst outside, whooping and hollering like a gunslinger exiting an Old West saloon.

Only difference was instead of a horse, there was Giuseppe and his Prius.

"Go, go, go," Rye needlessly shouted. And then, "faster, you turtle mother-fucker! Drive faster!"

"Stop bouncing, stay calm. I'm not going faster; I'm just going to drive."

"Fuck," Rye muttered in reply. "Goddamned Rain Man, my getaway driver."

A Corvette flew past them in the left lane. Even better, it was a bright yellow Corvette. Giuseppe immediately pulled in behind it and floored the gas pedal, soon cruising along at 75 mph.

"Hey, easy, Yertle," Rye mocked from the back seat. "I thought slow and steady won the race and all that shit."

"It does."

"Then why you flying now?"

"You see that Corvette?"

"Hard to miss it."

"It's not about going fast. It's about knowing *when* to go fast. If there's a cop up ahead, he's going to have to choose: pull over the Earth lover in the dented, scratched Prius or the rich, smug asshole in his bright, new Corvette. I'll tell you, son, 12 times out of 10, they pick the Corvette. Fast is not an action or a direction; it's a school of thought."

Rye sank back into the back seat and sighed. Getting this guy to talk was like taking a shit that wasn't ready. And when you did get him to say something, you didn't know what the hell he was saying.

They finished the trip in silence. Rye reveling in the shadowy glow of an Ur-crime gilded as *machismo*; Giuseppe lost in his patterns. For it was patterns primarily that Giuseppe liked, not people.

10

He didn't walk into a room so much as he drifted into it. The way a shadow would. For that's basically what Pollard was, a shadow. He was paid to clean up, to remove any trace of certainty, any rumor of identity, any hint of accountability. In the industry, they called it being a remora. Pollard never liked that word, found it suggested an imbalance, gave too much credit to the shark. He preferred the term, "eraser." That was more accurate. Other times, when he was feeling a slight bit whimsical—an indulgence he seldom allowed himself—he'd answer, when asked what he did, that he "worried. I'm a paid worrier."

And he did. He worried and he erased. Came in after a job and looked for the potential tells. The footprint, the button loosed free during a scuffle, the bullet casing, anything that could hint, insinuate, or whisper who did the job. Or even if a job had been done. Because of Pollard, to this day, people think Jimi Hendrix choked on his own vomit.

And the list of regular clients who needed or wanted erasing was quite the eclectic bag. The C.I.A., the *mafioso*, with their internecine strife, hitmen who were paid not just for the kill but for the added fear of anonymity, they all came calling on Pollard.

And so did Auguste Cameratto. Pollard had done some previous work for Cameratto over the years, had great respect for the former Commissioner, appreciated his even-keel (for his profession, at least), and so was quite happy to take the call and the job that followed the call.

It sounded like a simple job. Accompanying some hot-head local, a meth dealer Cameratto had a business relationship with, as he "tied up loose ends," which in this case meant whacking some civilian who sat on the wrong bench at the wrong time.

Cameratto's driver, Giuseppe, was stoic at the wheel, and Pollard didn't have much to say to this boaster punk, who called himself "Rye"—"you know, like the whiskey." Even if Pollard was inclined, it would have been hard to get a word in edge-wise, the stream of braggart word-vomit coming from the kid's mouth as he tried to establish his *bona fides* as a fellow tough guy, completely ignorant that actual tough guys have no concern for *bona fides*.

"We're here," Giuseppe broke into the interminable blathering, pulling up beside an apartment complex.

If anything, the kid got more braggadocious. The false façade of a shallow soul masquerading as hardcore experience. A part of Pollard began to regret taking the job.

"Just do the job. In and out. Be quick and be thorough," Pollard told him. "Stop acting like this is a movie, and just get it done. You linger, you embellish, and you get caught, *capice*?"

"Yeah, yeah, I got it," Rye said.

Pollard's phone rang. "Hold on, kid," he said as he flipped it open.

On the other side of the phone, Cameratto said, "Change in plan. We're going to do that other thing, instead. *Just* the other thing. You understand?"

"Yes, *Signore*. I understand."

"Please. Auguste," Cameratto said before hanging up.

"Change in plan," Pollard said to the other two. "We're going to the other location first."

"Why are we doing that," the kid whined.

"Because the boss said so."

When they arrived at the "other location"—a root cellar on a seemingly long-abandoned farm—about forty minutes later, Pollard let the kid go first. Not just because the kid was so eager to be a tough guy, but because it allowed him to screw the sound suppressor onto his Beretta 92-S without the kid noticing. And it made it much easier to put two rounds into the back of the kid's skull.

To tie up loose ends.

11

Carter watched Violet hug her grandfather on the front porch. The car idled in front, the taciturn driver leaning against it, waiting, like Carter, to continue on. Carter assumed the driver was far less puzzled than he was. He had no problem admitting to his confusion, nor to the fear that laced it. He had been told from childhood that "real men" dismissed such things, hid them, denied their daily presence, but Carter had spent too much of his time confused, and more time than he'd like to admit slightly afraid, so that lesson never made much sense to him. Confusion and fear, it seemed to him, were too essential a component of life to deny. Like running a three-legged race with two different partners. Because he understood this about confusion and fear in time, there was a chance he'd make it. Or he might not. Who knew?

But admitting one's confusion is not the same as negotiating one's way through it. Carter found no clarity on the ride from OKC to Krebs. For the entire two-hour trip, the driver said nothing. The only explanation—such as it was—he got was a brief call from Violet a few minutes in. All she told was that everything was OK, that she'd see him when he got "here."

And now he was "here." But no closer to understanding why.

Her good-byes said, Violet slid into the car's back seat, and Carter followed. Auguste Cameratto leaned into the open window, addressed Carter, "I have some business associates. And things are a little tense between us at the moment. The younger brother did some things he shouldn't have. So, I had to address that. The older brother seems more reliable, and I think he gets it. But who can tell? Family, and all, right? So I want my granddaughter to go somewhere safe for the time being. And I want you to go with her?"

"But why me?" Carter could have kicked himself after, questioning the very thing he had wanted since he and Violet were kindergarteners.

"Violet speaks highly of you," Cameratto replied. "Has for quite a long time. Sometimes," here Cameratto shifted his gaze towards his granddaughter, "it takes us awhile to see what's right in front of us."

Cameratto knew he wasn't telling the kid enough. But he told him enough. He didn't need to know the inexplicable timing of Natrillo delivering the accident report from Roma's, in which Cameratto read the name of the busboy who saved him, the same name Cameratto gave Pollard a half-an-hour before, the same name Violet has mentioned since she was in kindergarten.

No, Cameratto did not give the kid everything. He gave him Violet. And that was enough. That was everything.

"*Meglio tardi chem ai*, as they say."

"Thank you, Mr. Cameratto," Carter said.

"Please. Auguste."

They drive in silence for a while. Then, sensing that Carter needed something more, Violet offered: "What can I say? I'm just one letter shy of 'violent,'"

From the front seat, Giuseppe broke his inexorable silence. "We're all just one letter away from violent. In an alphabet we don't understand."

After few beats of additional silence, he added, "Where to, Violet?"

"Just drive, Giuseppe," she answered. "Just Drive."

12

Hans breathed deep, filling his lungs with invigorating alpine air. Off in the distance, cumulus shrouded the shoulders of Mont Tendre, its peak seemingly floating on a table of cloud.

Hans took another deep breath and thought how good life was. Behind and underneath him, the Large Hadron Collider did its thing, as it has for two, blissfully-incident-free years. He had the evening to himself. He thought he'd maybe walk around the lake. He never got tired of staring at the *Jet d'Eau*, letting it harmonize with his spirit, itself blithe and incident-free. Then maybe walk up one of Geneva's steep hills, decide on one of his favorite bistros.

Hans was in a delightful mood. The phone call with his son, Andre, had brought wonderful news. He was an understudy no more. The actor he was behind (Alex—Hans thought Andre said his name was Alex) had been discovered in the Canadian River, just outside OKC. Multiple gunshot wounds. "Perforated," was the word Andre used. And as a result of this random, haphazard event, his son would receive his big break, was understudy no more. Hans was delighted, proud. Insisted Andre send him a Playbill from his first performance.

Later, at the lake's edge, watching the plume of water shoot 140 meters skyward, momentarily blending with the atmosphere from which it came, Hans thought about the randomness of the world. The sheer potential of and within coincidence. That's why he loved what he did, working on the Hadron Collider, finding meaning out of random collisions. Particles collide, and things happen. Just like life.

He remembers all the worry, all the fear when the project finally went online. So many people worried about the implications, the so-called risks. There were some who even thought that turning on the Large Hadron Collider would be an end-of-the-world event, a sheer catastrophe of galactic proportions. It would create a black hole on Earth, some fantasists decried, swallowing up all life as we knew it.

Hans still scoffs at such foolishness. Nothing but childish confusion and fear. Any risk involved was statistically less-likely (significantly so, in fact) than a broken condom. The Hadron Collider was no more dangerous, involved no more risk, than sitting on a park bench.

Truth or Consequences

I shall be telling this with a sigh
Somewhere ages and ages hence
                    Robert Frost

Iggy Pop tried his best to save us.

We were already into our second hour of uncomfortable quiet, the strained silence of an abandoned battlefield. And we were still 240 miles from our destination. She sat, pressed against the passenger door as if recoiling from a leper, which, in her mind, I suppose I was. Her arms folded tightly across her chest, her mouth twisted into a calcified moue. I'm sure I looked no better, no more accommodating. I like to think when annoyed, frustrated, my jawline set rigid and rugged, that I look steely and tough, like Tom Selleck did on *Magnum P.I.* back when I was a kid, like Tom Selleck still tries to do today on whatever that show is now. But I strongly suspect back then I just looked silly, over-inflated and petulant. As we do.

We might very well have stayed that way the rest of the trip, rolling into Truth or Consequences a little before dusk, just in time to check into the hotel before catching the sunset and sharing an ice-cold beer before the routine frolicking pleasures of the bed. At least, that had been our plan. Now, I doubted we'd even glance at the sunset, would not give the roiling oranges and boiling purples, would barely give the churning cauldron of the sky a passing thought before we broke that cardinal rule of relationship experts the world over: not to go to bed angry.

We might very well have stayed this way. Isolated, encased in animus. But that's when Iggy Pop decided to help.

There's something prophetically threatening about the controlled chaos that opens his "Lust for Life." Those drums, primal and bubbling, some gigantic beast running down (or perhaps up, who knew?) an off-stage stairwell intent on destruction, the looming, threatening promise of the Johnny Yen of the song's opening line, all seemed as good a soundtrack to where we were as a couple as anything else.

But when she broke the silence, singing the chorus, inexplicably, as "Let's Go Live," the ice inside me thawed and I broke out laughing.

"What?" she demanded.

I couldn't answer, the laughter had seized its own momentum and would not release its grip for anything as mundane as words.

"What?" she demanded again. "What the hell are you laughing at?"

While I tried to gather myself, to regain the necessary composure to navigate this unexpected mine field, I reached down into the side panel of the driver's side door and pulled out the jewel case. I handed it over and with my finger tapped just below track 18.

"It's 'Lust for Life'; not 'Let's Go Live.'"

The moue returned, but more elastic this time.

"So? How was I supposed to know? Guy just growls and mumbles."

"Bad Iggy! Bad Boy! Yeah, I don't know how he lives with himself."

"Fuck off," Janie said, the hint of a smile breaking through, the faintest hint of that seductive purr creeping ever so slowly back into her voice. "Remember Donny?" she asked.

Donny, my perineal fuck-up of a roommate the last three semesters of college, where Janie and I met, began our Olympian frolics. Donny, man, I haven't seen him in over a year now. Hadn't thought of him in at least as long.

Janie would have to bite down on a bandana so Donny wouldn't hear us (or hear us that well) when we'd retreat to the bedroom.

"What made you think about him?"

A dark-gray storm cloud floated just to the left of the horizon.

"How he would always get that Jimi Hendrix song wrong. Remember? He'd always sing 'Excuse me while I kiss this guy'?"

Now that it was aimed elsewhere, our laughter blended, and the spell broke. Sunsets and beer and frolics seemed back on the menu.

When the laughter subsided, I placed a hand on her warm thigh, a mute peace offering. She placed hers on top of it, in mute acceptance.

"And then there's you," Janie said.

"What about me?"

She pulled her sunglasses down, looked at me over the rims.

"'Hold me closer, Tony Danza'?"

"I thought Elton John was a fan of *Who's the Boss*."

"You do know the song was released in '71?"

"Maybe Elton John's a wizard. I don't know. What can I say? I'm just as God made me. Just a flawed human being."

Janie squeezed my hand tighter, slid it, in preview, a little higher. And the seductive purr was back now, full force.

"Aren't we all? Glory, glory, hallelujah, aren't we all?"

That was us, two flawed human beings, driving across southern New Mexico, in search of Truth or Consequences. We weren't sure which.

***

The *first* fight—not the one that produced the two-hour freeze—was, if I'm being honest, my fault. We had decided to celebrate the close of our first full year in graduate school, where we let the momentum of undergraduate degrees in English Lit propel us towards a Master's degree in the same, with a road trip. For a few days after this decision, we didn't have a place in mind. We only knew we'd go west. Towards the promise of the horizon. Perhaps it was mere whim, perhaps the fanciful glance at the atlas, her eyes catching the name of the town, that made Janie push for Truth or Consequences. I think if the name of the town was more compound, less suggestive of an option, a choice, an either/or, we would have kept looking.

But it wasn't, and we didn't.

We took a month to save up for the trip, and then left from Ft. Worth in early June. Like most young couples moving out of the "constant-fucking" relationship phase, into the constant-fuck-ing-but-now-sensing-there-may-be-more-here" relationship phase, we used the early miles of the drive to prod beneath each other's surface. Perhaps it was the dynamic movement of the car, a motion that is implicitly suggestive of erasure, of the possibility of retracing and trying again if a wrong turn is made, or perhaps it was our unified movement through the alien landscape of red rock and canyon in west Texas that leant a surreal, impermanent quality to our conversations, that dispelled, with profound prejudice, the idea of taboo.

Whatever it was, we discussed topics we would never have felt comfortable discussing across the patio table we kept on the balcony and where we ate all of our meals—the dining room of the apartment repurposed into a library/study—or in the post-coital embrace of the bedroom.

Would we ever consider doing porn? Should we become swingers? What were our most scandalous, most shameful fantasies? We didn't reach definitive conclusions on these topics, but because we were young and flushed, the subjects titillated us, consumed by the idea that love meant doing anything for the other.

Looking back on that early portion of the road trip, I have to laugh that it wasn't talk of threesomes or moresomes, voyeurism or water sports that provoked the first fight; that it was the silly game we decided to play after, Janie's rather harmless question the game provoked.

Playing off the name of our destination, we decide to fill the stretch of desolate landscape west of Lubbock playing "Truth or Dare." I spent my first passes as one would expect, fueling my overstimulated libido with dares to flash me, then to remove her panties. Things were progressing nicely and I was planning my next turn, the clichéd blow-job-while-driving dare, already anticipating that warm wetness.

"You know, the game is called *Truth* or Dare, not Dare," Janie complained mildly. "It's no fun when it's just Dare. The balance is what keeps it fresh and fun."

"OK. It's your turn. Do you want to go with Truth?"

"I do." She paused for dramatic effect. "You do like country music, don't you?"

We had been alternating CDs on the trip, and with every turn, Janie popped in one of an amalgamated assortment of talentless cookie-cutter country crooners. If it weren't for the ability to sneak a glance at the jewel cases, I would have no way to know the difference between Blake Shelton, Brad Paisley, or Kenny Chesney. I had just finished a white-knuckled pass through a series of indistinguishable songs from Alan Jackson when she asked, so certainly the timing was against me.

In the early days, when you'll say anything, I assured Janie that despite my obvious bent towards classic rock of the 70s, and the edgier push of 90s rock, that I was also a huge country music fan. Who wasn't? And, since one is required to submit evidence from time to time, I parleyed a relative tolerance for Travis Tritt into proof when proof was required. Put *Down the Road I Go* on my Christmas list one year, would belt out "Modern Day Bonnie and Clyde" at karaoke.

Like I said before, that first fight was my fault. I should have known better. The idea that relationships must be built on full and total transparency and complete honesty, is a myth. A pretty damaging one at that. Relationships can—no, I'll say it stronger—*should* be built with a healthy dose of small dishonesties, of knowing which hills are worth fighting for and which ones aren't.

I should have known better. Should have said, "yes, honey, I do." Kept peppering in Travis Tritt, maybe subtly steered us toward a common ground of the singer/songwriter phase, strategically placed Townes van Zant or Willie Nelson on future Christmas lists, and moved on into predictable bliss.

But I didn't. Caught up in the *zeitgeist* of full disclosure and openness the trip had instilled in us, I answered truthfully, with consequences.

The *second* fight—not the one that produced the two-hour freeze—was, if I'm being honest, my fault. After her response to my answer, it was clear that any more "Dare" fun was on hold, at least for a while. So I was left with silence or Truth. I should have chosen silence.

"My turn. Truth. You ever sleep with Donny?"

It was a stupid question. I did not yet understand that the things she was willing to do in the bedroom, the things she was willing to try, was a function of her concept of love, not a function of her character.

Fortunately, the absurdity of the question subsumed any offense she might have taken.

"Donny? You must be joking?"

"Yeah," I nervous-laughed. "I am totally joking. Your turn."

Janie was silent for a stretch. It was not the silence of question forming; it was the silence of internal debate, of asking oneself if they should ask.

"Truth. How many kids do you think we'll have?"

Her question floored me, for, if I'm being honest, I thought we had covered this topic before. Covered it extensively and conclusively. I thought she understood.

I did not want to have kids. Ever. I think a lot of kids who grow up with a shitty parent have the other one to provide some balance. I had two shitty parents. I had no model for what effective parenting would look like. Again, if I'm being honest, the idea of parenting scared the shit out of me, and early on I decided I wouldn't take the risk of producing someone as wounded as I was. Or worse, God forbid.

Whenever the subject came up, I told her this. And she agreed. Said she also did not want to have children. In the early days, you'll say anything.

I thought, based on all the stories I had told her, she should have expected my answer (but then again, they weren't *her* stories; they were mine). But she didn't. And the answer clearly wounded her, offered a competing narrative about us that she didn't want to consider, one that threatened to uproot all the myths she believed in.

She did her best to hide her disappointment. But certain stings cannot be hidden.

As you move through the Lincoln National Forest on Rt. 82, you come through a tunnel. On the other side is an astonishing view of staggering beauty. To the right, a steep crag in the earth, a narrow, pine-lined canyon within which raptors vector. Your forward gaze takes in the descent down the Sacramento Mountains into the white-sand valley below. A breath-taking slide towards the horizon is promised. Many would posit this as an apt metaphor for love, for the culmination of the development, of the integration of soul mates. This is also a myth. There are no soul mates. There are only fellow travelers. And that is good enough.

Myth or not, Janie and I stopped here anyway.

The major fight and Iggy's rescue behind us, we took in the view, let its promise-laden mountain air fill our lungs. We were safe within the thinking of our own thoughts. I felt no need to share mine. Janie did.

"Did you know they pair for life," she asked, pointing at a hawk floating below us within the chasm. I didn't know then if that was true. I still don't. But I didn't dispute the point; wouldn't have known how to even if I wanted. And I didn't point out the dead and flattened hawk on the highway's shoulder, killed by an inability to adjust to its preconceived notions, to a world now made up of asphalt and motor vehicle.

The *final* fight—the one Iggy Pop saved us from—was, if I'm being honest, both of our faults. She should not have asked the question; I should not have answered. She wanted a promise. I could not give one.

One day I was in a rush to get to work, caught a yellow light, which, in turn meant a few intersections later, I was stuck while a train oozed laborious across the road, blocking my way, delaying my preconceived path. The pause filled with thoughts novel and unexpected. I thought about the life now adjusted by an altered timeline, one certainly different from what would have been if I missed the yellow. How many lives have I missed by living this one?

One does not think this way if they are in love.

I don't remember much of what we did once we got to Truth or Consequences. I imagine we watched sunsets and drank ice-cold beer. And because we were still young and flush enough to be willing to put off seriousness until tomorrow to have fun today, I'm sure we frolicked plenty.

It's the trip I remember when I think of Janie. And I do think of her from time to time, especially when Iggy Pop finds his way onto the airwaves. The seeds of our breakup were planted on that trip.

She wanted love. I thought I had it to give her. In hindsight, what I felt was something more akin to gratitude. After all those years of being told through word and deed that I was not quite lovable, by the very people who are supposed to love unconditionally, Janie noticed me, upended the narrative of my childhood. And I am thankful for that.

But gratitude could only have taken us so far. Routine would have settled into our lives like water in a pneumoniac's lungs. The inertia of habit would take over, bury us, until one day we would wake to discover bitter souls within us, with only one place to lay down sudden and terrifying blame.

I remember a minor disagreement we had on that road trip, before the cracks Iggy tried to repair. We had reached Artesia. I wanted to head south, toward the caverns of Carlsbad. Janie wanted to keep west, stick to the original plan. It's hard not to see this moment as a crossroads of sorts. I try not to ascribe symbolic significance to this moment, to view my preference for the caverns as signifying that I was deeper than her, or that Janie's preference to stay on the surface made her superficial. These would be trite conclusions, self-serving and untrue. All it means is we wanted to go in different directions. But, of course, that means everything.

She wanted the myth. A soul mate, kids, the white-picket fence, a neatly-trimmed yard. Weekends spent working the flower bed. Vacations at Cape May. I couldn't give her that. It would have been a kind of Hell for me. Love isn't about *doing* anything for someone; it's about *being* anything for someone. And I wasn't willing to be that for Janie. A caged bird only sings in hopes you'll someday let it out, not because it enjoys the song. Out here, where I am now, you don't have lawns; you have land. Endlessly stretching to a horizon. All yours for the viewing.

On the way home from that trip, I remember we found ourselves on a winding mountain pass. There were no guardrails. The drop, seemingly inches from the passenger side door, was sheer, whispering of the fatal solemnity of one slip. But the view was spectacular, literally breathtaking. We were both filled with awe and fear.

In the decades since, driving across the state, north and south, east and west, I have never been able to find this particular stretch of road again. I thought it was near Tucumcari, but it has eluded recapture. Of course, I may be wrong, my memory of it unreliable. Maybe it was in Texas. I do not know; I cannot be sure. What I do know is that there are other spectacular views. All of them solemn, all of them breathtaking. I have seen them. I hope to see more.

And maybe I'll see some of them with someone else, for whom I will be willing. I haven't found that person yet. Maybe never will. It's taken me a lot of years to understand that that's okay. It's enough to have a lust for life.

If I'm being honest, I don't regret that it didn't work out with Janie. But I do feel—strongly—that the town should change its name to Truth *and* Consequences. Because they go hand-in-hand.

Where the Wild Things Were

"But you, O my brothers, remember sometimes
thy little Alex that was. Amen."
A Clockwork Orange

We used to call it wilding, until current events took
that name away from us. A bunch of suburban teenagers let
loose each summer night, sneaking through the yards of
unsuspecting neighbors.

Sometimes our exploits were merely annoying.
Bags of cut grass sliced open and dumped back on
lawns—prodigals returned. Or the rail part of some
would-be horse baron's (a fleet of Mercedes standing in for
the horses) post and rail fence removed, rearranged to spell
some sophomoric vulgarity across his lawn.

Sometimes our exploits were arbitrarily destructive.
Landscaping rocks, some of them the size of car tires,
thrown or rolled into pools, pools that had the audacity to
be in-ground. Or the time Marc and I took down another
rail from another poser's post and rail, and ran down the
side of the street with it over our shoulders,
battering-ramming every mailbox off its stanchion, Freddie
following in our wake, pulling each red flag off, because he
wanted a collection. He also pulled off every "6" and "9"
for reasons he did not have to explain.

Sometimes our exploits were merely criminal. An
unlocked car, or backyard shed, the whispered frenzied
bartering as each took what they wanted.

Sometimes our exploits were quite clever, like the
time Mr. Paddock had a new sod lawn put down one
August morning. We came by that night to roll it up again,
carried the rolls behind his house. I no longer remember
whose idea it was to pen a quick note that read, "Your front
lawn is now your back lawn," but I thought that was a nice
touch.

But sometimes our exploits had a more focused target, a more focused meaning. Sometimes our general dissatisfaction, our addled, formless rage congealed into a more narrowed revenge, an acting out of a specific grievance against a specific martinet. Like the time Mr. Anderson told me I did not do a good enough job cutting his lawn and he would find someone else to do it. For this unwarranted act, I stood one night on the hood of his BMW, pissed down the air ducts to the stifled cheers and applause of my friends. Now, when Mr. Anderson fired up his air conditioning to fight back the oppressive New England summer humidity, he'd get a faceful blast of urine stink. An apt penance for taking away a $15/week gig. He's lucky he kept his car locked.

It was one of those revenge nights when Jimmy (I think it was Jimmy) brought a sack of fireworks and told the horde to follow him. He led us over to Dogwood Lane, gathered us in a copse of pine on one side of the cul-de-sac and handed out bottle rockets. He had matchbooks as well, but, of course, we all already had lighters. He told us not to light the fuses until he gave the signal. He ran across the street, rang a doorbell, put his ear against the door, and then gave us the signal. And laughed the rest of the night and most of the next week about the man who answered his door to a hail of rockets.

We did this several times over the next few months, at haphazard intervals. We found it hilarious. Especially the last time before the last time. When the timing was not quite right, and the man stood in the doorway for several beats while the fuses burnt down. He just stood there. He must have heard the hiss of potassium nitrate and sulfur burning down. But he just stood there. He must have recognized, must have understood what was coming. But he just stood there. Framed in the glow of his lighted doorway. He just stood there. "Oh, Jesus," he whined out into the darkness. And stood there, awaiting the barrage of bottle rockets.

It was the "Oh, Jesus" that got us, that had us rolling with laughter the second we got to safety (some of us couldn't hold out, laugh-ran the whole way, straggling in behind the others). Those words, that voice—not of despair, for it went deeper than that; it was the hopelessness of it, its bleak pathos, sounding out the full futility of angst—made us delirious with mirth. How pathetic, we hooted. How truly pathetic.

We never knew (or at least I didn't) what this man did to Jimmy (if it *was* Jimmy). We never thought to ask, for it did not matter. We branded these acts as a pushing back, a striking out against the discontent of our hermetically-sealed suburban lives. We were young.

We had no way of knowing what would happen next. No way of knowing that one of us (maybe Jimmy, maybe someone else caught up in the seduction of one-up-manship, of the feverish unfettered freedom of not simply line-crossing, but refusing to acknowledge lines have purpose, have weight or existence). We had no way of knowing it was just a matter of time before one of us took the next logical step. We all had lighters. We were young. Potassium nitrate and sulfur were not the only things that burn down.

In the decades since, I think back to the last time before the last time. Of that man standing illuminated in his doorway, knowing what was coming. I've wondered why he never shut the door. If he heard the burning fuses, recognized once again the set-up, why didn't he turn around and shut us out? Why did he just stand there? Why, in the face of this unreasoning, arbitrary malice, did he just offer up that pathetic, "Oh, Jesus," and take it?

I've thought about this a lot. As I sit on my porch at night, my hands and arms cross-hatched with scars, the pendulum swings of certain self-tribunal. Waiting. I am old now. Frail. All around me in the dark is vigor. Addled and formless vigor. Wilding. Striking out at its discontent. Its judgment is severe and inevitable. It rejects the false abated apology of Burgess's last chapter. Embraces the inexorable terror of Kubrick's restoration. I used to wonder why that man never shut the door. I am old now. And frail. Now I know.

Acknowledgments

The list of people I need to thank for this collection of short fiction, parts of which have been the labor of seven years and more, is long and I will undoubtedly overlook some of you. Please know that this is the effect of a poor memory and not a lack of gratitude.

That said, I would like to thank Hank Jones, Jeanetta Calhoun Mish, Allison Amend, Tim Bradford, Kerry Cohen, Ky George, Danielle DeFoe, Cullen Whisenhunt, Keely Record, Mindy Choate, Woodstok Farley, and Liz Blood for lending their time and attention to some or all of these stories as they sluggishly moved their way through the revision process. Your collective sharp eyes and kind, supportive feedback were essential to this collection seeing the light of day.

I would like to thank the editors of *Concho River Review* for first publishing "Appalachian" (after fourteen rejections) and the editors of *Main Street Rag* for first publishing "A Dirge for Griffin Morris" (after ten rejections) and to the editors of *The Oklahoma Review* for publishing "Here Be Monsters." There is every chance I might have given up on this collection without these reaffirmations.

I would like to thank Woodstok Farley (again), Drew Geyer, Rilla Askew, Rob Roensch and Christopher Murphy for offering their kind and thoughtful words about this collection.

I would like to thank Roxie Kirk and *Fine Dog Press* for her tireless work on this, and for her unflagging efforts to advance the writing community of Oklahoma.

I would like to thank the writing community of Oklahoma for existing, and for existing the way you exist.

I would like to thank Oklahoma, for the same reasons.

But mostly, I would like to thank Ky George (again). The dedication is not hyperbole. A debt only the shadow of which can ever be repaid.

About the Author

Living what could be charitably called a nomadic life, Paul Juhasz was born in western New Jersey, grew up just outside New Haven, Connecticut, and has spent appreciable chunks of his life in the plains of central Illinois, in the upper hill country of Texas, and in the Lehigh Valley in Pennsylvania. Most recently seduced by the spirit of the red earth, he now lives in Oklahoma City. A graduate of the Red Earth M.F.A., his work has appeared in several literary journals, most recently *Concho River Review, Poetry Quarterly, Oklahoma Review* and *Main Street Rag*. He has been serving as curator and coordinator of the Woody Guthrie Poets since 2020. His first book, *Fulfillment: Diary of a Warehouse Picker*—a mock journal covering his six-month stint in an Amazon warehouse—was published by Fine Dog Press in 2020. His second book, *Ronin*, a collection of (mostly) prose poems—also published by Fine Dog Press—was named a finalist for the 2022 Oklahoma Book Award in poetry. His second collection of poetry, *The Inner Life of Comics*, was published by Turning Plow Press in the fall of 2022.